Waves Break My Fall

Kendall McKenna

Published by KMB Press, 2024.

WAVES BREAK MY FALL

First edition. July 23, 2024.

ISBN: 979-8227932556

Written by Kendall McKenna.

Table of Contents

Waves Break My Fall

Kage is a Marine, newly returned from Iraq and having difficulty adjusting to being home. He tries to decompress with a quiet, solo trip to Puerto Vallarta.

Zach is newly graduated from college and facing the realities of adulthood and beginning his new career. Their mutual attraction is immediate and intense. Zach is undemanding and seems to understand what Kage is going through. Kage has the physical strength that Zach desires, as well as the strength of character to let him be his own man.

Their summer vacation romance sizzles, but when the time arrives for Zach to return home, will either of them be willing—or able—to walk away?

Dedication

I give my undying gratitude to the United States Marine Corps. Through their dedication, loyalty, intensity, and fighting spirit, they have defended the country we share. They have also managed to engage my imagination. In addition to ensuring my safety and security, they have provided me with colorful characters and intriguing drama to write about. While I am sure I would never run short of story ideas, it is a joy to write about bad-ass Marines falling in love.

The Marines I have seen around the world have the cleanest bodies, the filthiest minds, the highest morale, and the lowest morals of any group of animals I have ever seen. Thank God for the United States Marine Corps!
—Eleanor Roosevelt, First Lady of the United States, 1945

FORWARD

Waves Break My Fall was originally released in July of 2012, by *Silver Publishing*. Not long after, the owner of that press admitted being in breach of contract. During the previous nine to twelve months, he collected all royalty payments from secondary sales distribution sites, then willfully and knowingly withheld royalties owed to contracted authors by *Silver Publishing*. He freely admitted to spending the monies owed to the authors on personal trips and possessions. He also used the author's royalties to fund recreational travel for the staff of *Silver Publishing*, which the staff knowingly accepted. *Silver Publishing* is now defunct, the owner having fled the United States without paying a large number of authors the thousands of dollars in royalties owed to them.

In October of 2012, the owner of *Silver Publishing* - per the terms of the author contracts - agreed to return publishing rights of individual books to the authors, upon request. With all trust in *Silver Publishing* (and its owner) destroyed, I demanded – and received – the publishing rights back for two books. One of those titles was **Waves Break My Fall.**

At that time, I chose not to immediately re-release **Waves** through my new publisher, but to revise it extensively before making it available once again. This revised edition of **Waves Break My Fall** contains an additional 20,000 words. Both Kage and Zach are more fully developed characters. This version of the story continues on with the day-to-day lives of these characters, as they adjust to being a new couple, and at the same time they must overcome some emotional difficulties. The original version of **Waves** remains intact; nothing has been removed from the 2012 edition. This revised update will be familiar to those who read it at the time of its original release but is most definitely an entirely new story.

Readers who enjoyed the original release version of **Waves Break My Fall** will love this second, expanded, and revised edition. If this revised edition is your first experience with **Waves**, rest assured, nothing is missing, or been removed. I'm confident everyone will enjoy getting to know Kage and Zach, as they get to know one another.

Kendall McKenna
November 2014

CHAPTER ONE

The taxi pulled to the curb on the first block of the Malicon. Ahead for five or six blocks stretched bars, restaurants, pharmacies, and knick-knack shops that comprised the central tourist area of Puerto Vallarta. Kage tossed a bunch of crumpled bills onto the front seat and climbed out. It was summer in Mexico, and the humid heat of Puerto Vallarta slammed into him like a wall, stealing his breath. Already, denim stuck to his legs and he wished he'd worn shorts. His white tank top and sandals at least mitigated the heat.

Kage was looking for a specific type of bar for his night of drinking, and he'd know it when he saw it. As he made his way down the sidewalk, he struggled not to flinch each time he was jostled by innocent passersby. He reminded himself for the thousandth time, that he was no longer in Iraq.

Nearly reaching the last block of the Malicon, Kage finally found a place that felt right—Surf Shack. He snorted. The décor was straight out of a 1960's beach-blanket movie. Cartoon sea life was painted on the walls and decorative surfboards hung throughout.

Just as he stepped inside, a loud noise sounded from the beach across the street. It echoed down the block, bouncing off of the building fronts. Kage startled violently. He ducked his head and shoulders, nearly dropping into a crouch. He searched reflexively for cover, even as his brain told him there was no real threat. Kage glanced around, relieved that no one seemed to notice his strange behavior.

Inside, the music was typically loud. It roared over Kage, deafening him, thundering through his bones. A circular bar stood off to the right. A handful of customers sat drinking quietly, watching the writhing and gyrating dancers. The small dance floor on the far side of the bar was filled with sweaty bodies. Up a split flight of stairs, a second dance floor was nearly as packed. The place was perfect.

Kage took in his surroundings as he approached the bar. He marked both exits. He sized up all the drinkers for potential threats, quickly dismissing most of them as nothing more than happy drunks. There was one guy Kage decided to keep an eye on. He had an angry expression and a tense set to his shoulders that made him look like he might be a belligerent drunk. The one bartender looked friendly. The crowds on the dance floors looked exultant and not aggressive. Kage rolled his shoulders, trying to ease the built-up tension.

Shouting over the music, he ordered a Pacifico. Kage unclenched his hands and slid some money from the front pocket of his jeans. He took the sweating bottle and moved to a bar-height table in the corner, leaning against it and hoping he looked relaxed. Kage had all entrances and exits in sight, as well as the seething crowd itself. Halfway through his beer, his muscles finally began to release their tense hold. Kage ran his hand over his light brown hair. He'd let it grow out some. He scratched at his cheek, the three-day growth of his beard was coarse under his nails. He was a week into thirty days of leave, and he'd told the grooming standard to go fuck itself. Kage knew he no longer resembled the Marine Gunnery Sergeant he was.

His second beer was icy in touch and taste. It was soothing. The ocean breeze couldn't reach him inside, so it was hotter in here than out on the street. Kage was already starting to sweat through the cotton of his tank top. He wished again, he'd worn shorts.

Kage clasped the neck of his beer loosely in his fingers as he leaned his elbows on the table behind him. He could finally watch the mass of dancing people with interest instead of caution and distrust. It was an unfamiliar sensation, not being constantly on the lookout for danger.

Glancing at the upper level, Kage watched the writhing crush of dancing bodies part to reveal a beautiful young man. Kage frowned and glanced around the bar again, looking closer at the occupants. Kage suddenly felt so fucking old. He was easily ten years older than everyone else in this place.

What the hell had possessed him to come here?

His eyes were drawn again to the guy on the upper dance floor. He seemed to be dancing with an entire group—the boys as well as the girls—rather than a single partner. He was lithe and graceful but unquestionably masculine. His shoulders and chest were broad, tapering into a trim waist and narrow hips. The thick muscles of his arms bunched and flexed with his every movement. Kage's cock shifted in his jeans, showing interest despite his brain's misgivings. The guy's face was flushed with the heat and exertion of his dancing. He smiled broadly at his companions, showing off perfectly straight, white teeth. His dark hair caught the dim lighting and shone burnished copper. Kage took a long drink of his beer and shifted his weight, trying to mask the way his dick pressed insistently against his zipper.

Just then, the guy glanced up from the woman who was shouting into his ear and looked right into Kage's eyes. When Kage didn't look away, the guy's grin grew into a wide smile.

Fuck.

Their impasse was broken only when the guy was jostled by the crowd. Kage drank down half of his beer in one go. Against his better judgment, he looked up at the second level again. The guy's back was to him now, his hips grinding into the girl pressed against him. Something hot flared in Kage's chest. His heart slammed against his ribs, and he couldn't catch his breath.

He was about to step to the bar for another beer when the guy released his dance partner and turned back to Kage. Struggling to keep anything from showing on his face, Kage watched the guy pull his tank top over his head and tuck it into the back pocket of his jeans.

Kage's mouth was dry with desire. His face might look young, but the guy's body belonged to a full-grown man. Kage could now see that tan skin covered those broad shoulders and a well-defined, muscular chest. The guy's cut abs were on full display as he gyrated around the dance floor to the pounding, pulsating beat of the music.

Pushing away from the table, Kage set his empty bottle on the bar with a jarring clunk, signaling the bartender for another. If the guy was going to put on a show, Kage would need more alcohol. He reminded himself he didn't have a shot in hell with someone like that. Especially not right now. Kage knew he was too rough around the edges, too coarse. He was difficult to get to know. Kage didn't talk a lot in the best of times, and now was not the best of times for him.

"Can I get a Corona?" asked a pleasantly masculine voice beside Kage.

He struggled not to flinch, realizing the music had masked the man's approach. It was something that could get him killed in Iraq, but he reminded himself again that he was no longer in Iraq.

Kage glanced over and froze, his heart leaping into his throat. The voice belonged to the hot guy from the dance floor. Kage was trapped by his startling green eyes. It was like the guy had been standing there, waiting for Kage to notice him.

"Hey," the guy greeted, the corner of his pouty lips lifting into a suggestive smile. His tank top was still tucked into his pocket, and Kage forced himself *not* to glance down at the guy's naked, sweaty chest.

"Hey," Kage replied, too stunned to return the smile. Gorgeous, well-groomed young men looking like they'd stepped out of a college catalog *did not* just start chatting Kage up.

The bartender set down a bottle of Pacifico and one of Corona. Hot Guy tossed down several bills. "That's for both," he said, grabbing the Corona and turning toward the table Kage had vacated. When he realized Kage wasn't following, Hot Guy turned back and shouted over his shoulder, "Coming?"

Kage took two long drinks of his beer and followed the guy like he'd been issued an order. He'd worry about that later.

Hot Guy set his beer on the table and pulled his tank top on over his head. Kage raked his gaze over the flex of muscle in his back as he moved, disappointed when his view became blocked by the tank top. Adjusting the hem of the shirt to his satisfaction, Hot Guy leaned one elbow on the table. Kage found himself mirroring the posture.

"Zach," the guy said, holding out his hand for Kage.

"Kage," he replied, impressed with the strength of Zach's grip, and his steady gaze. He found himself captivated by Zach's amber-flecked green eyes.

"Are you alone?" Zach queried "Or do you have friends who'll eventually catch up?"

"Nah, I came here by myself." Kage was annoyed at having to shout over the blare of the concussive music.

"Here to the bar or here to Mexico?" Zach took a long drink of his beer, and Kage admired his full lips wrapped around the opening of the bottle.

Cock aching, Kage dropped his eyes and watched Zach's throat work as he swallowed. "Uh, Mexico. I came to Mexico alone."

Zach nodded sagely, his mouth quirking in a way that said he knew the direction of Kage's thoughts.

"Did you just get back?"

"Get back?" Kage's brow furrowed with confusion.

"From the Middle East or wherever you were deployed?"

Kage's blood ran cold despite the tropical heat. He stared hard at Zach. He'd given nothing away that would have hinted at his military status.

"Why would you ask that?" He demanded, pulling himself up to his full height of six foot two inches. "Because of your—" Zach reached for Kage's neck.

Unable to mask his flinch this time, Kage pulled away abruptly. Zach snatched his hand back as if he'd been scalded.

"I'm sorry... I was just... your dog tags." Zach's expression showed surprise and confusion. He gestured toward Kage's chest.

Kage reached up and ran his fingers along his own neck, feeling the tiny beads of the ever-present stainless steel chain. He was chagrined. Glancing down, Kage saw the dark outline of his tags beneath the fabric of his tank top. They were made prominent by the black rubber silencers that kept them from clinking together.

Fuck. He didn't remember slipping them back on after his shower; it was such an ingrained habit.

"Sorry," Kage muttered, unsure what else to say to smooth over the sudden awkwardness. He shifted his weight anxiously.

"No, it was my bad," Zach said easily, waving off Kage's apology.

"Iraq." He blurted, feeling he owed Zach that much of an explanation. "Been back a week and a half." Kage leaned against the table again, feigning casualness he didn't feel and hoping his body would eventually cooperate.

"Shouldn't you be at home with your family and friends?" Zach's tone was incredulous. His eyes were open wide as he seemed to assess Kage.

Kage glanced around the room, looking at other customers, the garish decorations, the sweat-soaked dancers, anywhere but into Zach's shrewd eyes. He wanted to meet Zach's gaze, but he couldn't, any more than he could answer Zach's question.

"Hey, you wanna go outside and get out of this racket?" Zach's sudden question surprised Kage, even as it thrilled him.

"Yeah," he answered with a curt nod.

They each finished off their beers and headed for the door.

"Zach?" a woman's voice shouted over the music.

Kage turned to see Zach waving to one of his earlier dance partners. She was tall and curvaceous. Her long hair was blonde was bleached lighter by the Mexico sun. She looked at Zach, expectant and curious as he nodded his head toward the door. The woman looked like she wanted to talk, but Zach never stopped making his way toward the exit.

Stepping out into the night, Kage took a deep breath of the cool ocean air. The sudden lack of blaring music was a startling relief. He stood on the edge of the curb for several moments, just breathing.

"Let's go across the street." Zach's tone was light as he stepped off the curb, gesturing for Kage to follow. Once they reached the beach side of the street, they straddled the wall separating the sand from the sidewalk.

The breeze flowing off the ocean was soothing. Kage closed his eyes and turned his face into it. How many times had he wished for this kind of cooling breeze when he'd been battling through the desert? Kage heard Zach sigh heavily. "I never realize how loud the music is until I'm not in it anymore."

Now that they were outside and free of the excuse of any distractions, Kage realized his tactical error. Zach would ask him questions now; pry into Kage's life, trying to get him to talk about things he wanted left in the desert.

"How long have you been here?" Zach asked.

"Three days." Kage answered without thinking. Long enough to bronze his skin all over and get rid of the fucking farmer's tan. Long enough that his feet had lost the sick, gray look of boot rot.

"Me too." Zach's tone was light. "How long are you staying?

"Ten days." He'd wanted to stay longer, but it was Mexico in the summer. Maybe he could find a room at a different resort.

"A week." Zach replied. "I love Puerto Vallarta. My friends and I come here every summer."

"I come here every few years, too." Kage relaxed a little. This was a safe conversation; he could have this conversation.

"I probably won't make it back for a couple of years, though."
The regret in Zach's voice made Kage look at him questioningly.

"The responsibilities of adulthood are finally getting their hooks into me." Zach's self-deprecating grin was bright in the moonless night.

"Aren't you in college?"

"Not anymore. Graduated last month."

"Congratulations." Kage couldn't figure out what Zach was doing out here with him. Kage never had trouble getting laid; he just didn't seem able to attract the ones who made a habit of thinking.

"Thanks."

Kage thought the polite thing to do would be to ask what Zach's degree was in and where he'd gone to school. On the other hand, if Zach wanted Kage to know these things he could elaborate, which he wasn't doing.

He was frozen with indecision. When had he lost his ability to make simple decisions? While his thoughts swirled and he tried to figure out what to do with the handsome, quiet man who seemed interested in him, silence again settled over the two of them.

In his discomfort, Kage turned and looked out over the ocean again, at least what he could see of it in the dark.

"Kage."

He turned at the sound of his name. His breath caught in his chest at the sight of Zach leaning into the space between them. His face was half in shadow from the ambient street light. His eyes glittered intensely. Kage's gaze dropped to Zach's parted lips, fascinated again by their fullness.

As Zach slowly leaned even closer, Kage's heart pounded in his chest. He closed his eyes just as warm, soft lips pressed to his own. He found himself tilting inward toward Zach, kissing him back.

Disappointment flooded Kage as Zach pulled back with a soft, wet sound. He was reluctant to let the kiss end. He'd never experienced a kiss that gentle, that undemanding.

"I thought we should get that out of the way," Zach said with a mischievous grin.

"Why is that?" Kage's voice sounded distant to his own ears.

"So, we can stop wondering what it's like, stop wondering when it's going to happen, and just have a conversation."

Kage snorted a self-conscious laugh. Zach was amazingly perceptive.

"I'm still not much of a talker," Kage said quietly.

"I have the feeling you'll do just fine, once you relax." Zach chuckled.

"So... where did you go to college?"

"If you really want to know, I'll tell you. But is that really what you're dying to know about me?"

"Isn't that the kind of thing I'm supposed to ask? You tell me you just graduated, and I ask where you went to school and what you majored in."

"Is that what people do to you?" Zach asked softly. "Ask you what branch of the military you're in and how many people you've killed?"

Kage clenched his jaw and swallowed hard. He looked down at his hands, fisted on the wall in front of him. "Marines," he said in a rough voice. "Infantry. First Battalion, Fourth Marines."

"Impressive." Zach sounded genuine. "San Diego State."

Kage nodded once, acknowledging that he was familiar with Zach's alma mater.

"So, are you stationed at Camp Pendleton?" Zach inquired.

"Yeah." Kage bounced his knee nervously. "We're practically neighbors."

Zach laughed and the sound stopped Kage's breath. "It's only what? An hour drive from State to Oceanside? How have we never run into each other before now?"

"If I had known there were hot guys like you going to State, I would have moved further south." It was a lie. Kage knew the kind of handsome young men who attended college, and most had no interest in a man like him. "I don't want to talk about this shit," he blurted, surprising himself.

"All right," Zach replied smoothly. "Just tell me this, does your family and friends know where you are?"

He could detect only curiosity and concern in Zach's tone, so Kage answered, "No."

"Do they at least know you're okay?"

"Yeah. I called my mom when I got here to tell her I was safe. Then I shut off my phone and buried it in a drawer under my clothes."

Zach tilted his head to the side and regarded Kage intently. Kage felt exposed under his scrutiny. "Not ready for backyard barbecues, probing questions, and being called a hero?"

He stared hard at Zach, unable to comprehend how he could read Kage so easily. "Exactly."

"Understandable. So, what *do* you really want to ask me?"

Kage said the first thing that came to mind. "Are you willing to take a walk down the beach with me?

Maybe find someplace quiet and let me kiss you again?"

Zach was in motion even before he answered. "Yeah, I am."

Kage slid off the wall and followed Zach down to the surf where it lapped gently at the sand.

They stayed to the hard-packed sand, just out of reach of the waves. The din of the Malicon faded away behind them until it was no more than ambient noise. Kage finally thought of a hundred things he wanted to ask Zach, things he honestly wanted to know. The words stuck in his throat.

Zach didn't seem to mind Kage's silence, though. He strolled along, looking relaxed and happy, each time Kage snuck a glance at him. He realized Zach was tall, only an inch or two shorter than Kage.

His imagination filled with images of how easily they could become entwined with so little size difference between them.

Heat flooded Kage's face, even as his cock stirred, but he pushed those thoughts away. They hadn't even shared a real kiss yet. What if Zach lost interest before they got that far?

Kage was hyperaware of small groups and couples dotting the beach, so he led Zach well past them all, to a deserted stretch of sand. He moved before he could think himself out of it. Kage turned and blocked Zach's path, curling both hands around the back of his head. He brought their mouths together, swiping his tongue along the seam of Zach's lips. Kage anticipated surprise, possibly resistance. Instead, Zach moaned softly and melted against him.

Changing the angle of the kiss, Kage savored the feel of their tongues rubbing wetly against each other. Zach's arms came around him, his hands running up Kage's back, fingers digging hard into his shoulders. Pulling back to breathe, Kage dragged his teeth lightly along Zach's lower lip. Zach tasted faintly of beer and felt like wet heat.

Kage gasped when Zach's tongue lapped at his upper lip. He licked deep into Zach's mouth. Breathing heavily, Kage caught the enticing scents of sweat, cologne, and something warm and spicy that he suspected was all Zach. Kage reached around and firmly grasped Zach's ass, pulling him in tight. Their bodies were flush, pressed hard against each other as Kage circled his hips. Zach pushed his hands up under Kage's shirt, skimming up the skin of his back.

Kage groaned into Zach's mouth, arching into his hands. When Zach broke the kiss, Kage chased him, growling in frustration. Reluctantly, he released his hold on Zach's hips, lifting his arms so Zach could tug his shirt over his head.

Free of the fabric, Kage wrapped his arms back around Zach's body. He buried his face in Zach's neck, flicking his tongue along the pulse point. Zach moaned softly, tilting his head to give better access. Kage placed an open-mouthed kiss on Zach's moist, warm skin. He inhaled deeply, his cock growing harder at the scent of Zach's cologne mixed with that spicy musk.

With his hands and his mouth, Kage encouraged Zach to kneel. It was far easier than he'd anticipated. Zach eased down onto the sand, Kage eagerly following him. He pulled Zach's shirt over his head then guided him to lie back.

Kage covered Zach's body with his own. He gasped into Zach's mouth at the feel of warm, naked skin against his chest. Burying his fingers in Zach's hair, Kage held him steady for bruising kisses. Zach wrapped his legs around Kage's hips and slid his arms around Kage's back. Hesitantly, Kage pressed his fully hard cock against Zach. He moaned low in his throat when Zach eagerly pushed his own erection into Kage's hip.

A gentle breeze drifted over them, and Kage realized how overheated his skin was when he was suddenly chilled. A shiver ran through him, but it was as much desire for the man beneath him as it was the cool air.

Kage's head was clasped between Zach's hands, encouraging him tilt it back. He choked on his own breath when Zach licked along the pulse of his throat. Zach's breath was hot when he exhaled against the wet flesh. Kage's blood roared in his ears but was still drowned out by Zach's harsh breathing.

"Fuck!" Kage gasped at the feel of Zach's teeth sinking into his earlobe. His fingers clenched in Zach's hair when he dragged his tongue along the shell of Kage's ear.

Kage's chest heaved as he dragged in each breath. He lowered his head and bit into the joint at Zach's neck and shoulder. A violent shudder ran through Zach's frame, gooseflesh rising on his skin.

"Oh, Christ," Zach whispered against Kage's cheek.

Kage pressed his mouth to Zach's again. It was off-center with their desperation, wet and sloppy. Zach's hands left Kage's head and found his ass, gripping hard and pulling their hips together firmly. The pressure was excruciating. Kage's erection throbbed against his zipper. He ached to take himself out, to feel cool air and Zach's hands on his heated cock. Zach pressed against Kage, his erection equally hard.

Zach broke their kiss on a gasp. "I wanna touch you." He reached for the button of Kage's jeans.

It was like he read Kage's mind, and it was as scary as it was so very easy. "Yeah, okay." Pulling back slightly, Kage tried to help, to speed up freeing his cock from the tight confines of his clothing. They were both clumsy in their eagerness. Kage thought his own hands might be trembling.

Zach impatiently pushed Kage out of the way. Kage held his breath as Zach fumbled at his fly. When Kage's cock was finally out of his jeans and in the palm of Zach's hand, he shuddered at the firm touch. He couldn't move. His eyes slowly closed at the exquisite feel of Zach's hand on him. He held himself very still, struggling for control.

"God, you're hot," Zach said, sounding breathless.

Kage clenched his jaw as Zach stroked and squeezed him. He didn't understand the wonder in Zach's voice. He was just a rough, unshaven grunt.

Glancing down the length of their bodies, Kage blew out a breath at the sight of Zach's hands touching him. It was one of the hottest things he'd ever seen. He needed to touch Zach in the same way, to bring him the same pleasure.

Sitting back on his heels, Kage awkwardly tugged open Zach's fly. Easing Zach's erection into the open air, he stroked firmly and heard the low groan that told him he'd done it just right.

Propping himself on one elbow, Kage aligned their hard cocks, head to base, and wrapped his free hand around them both. One of Zach's hands joined his. Kage gave an experimental thrust of his hips. Fission raced up his spine and sparks exploded inside his skull. Beneath him, Zach flexed his hips, sliding their cocks against one another. The friction was almost unbearable. Zach slid his free hand beneath the waistband of Kage's jeans and grasped his ass, encouraging him to move.

Kage chanced a glance down at Zach, expecting him to have his eyes shut. He was surprised to find Zach watching him intently. His neck was arched, eyes glittering in the dim light from the street. Zach breathed heavily through his parted lips. He was fucking gorgeous, and he watched Kage hungrily. It didn't make sense.

Suddenly, Zach's eyes widened. "Oh, fuck," he groaned. "Don't stop Kage. Don't stop touching me."

Kage wouldn't dare. He pumped his hips against Zach's body, stroking their joined hands over their cocks. Zach trembled, coming apart beneath him.

Arching off the sand, Zach threw his head back, biting his lips to silence his cries. His free hand dug painfully into the thick muscles in Kage's back. Zach's cock pulsed in Kage's hand, ropes of hot come landing on his belly, running down over their twined fingers. He gasped loudly, easing back down into the sand but not releasing his grip on Kage's back or their joined cocks.

Zach's body vibrated as he rode the aftershocks of his orgasm, and Kage felt his own begin to build. Heat pooled low in his belly. His muscles clenched. He slammed his eyes shut as a light show played across the backs of his lids. Kage's cock swelled in their joined hands until his own come mingled with Zach's on bare skin.

They both lay for interminable moments, breathing harshly. Their gasps were loud, even over the sounds of the wind and surf. Kage was completely wrung out. He wanted to collapse onto Zach, press his face into sweaty skin, and breathe him in. This was just a hand job on a beach in Mexico, Kage told himself, now was not the time to get clingy.

Kage sat up and reached for his discarded tank top with a shaky hand.

"Use mine," Zach said in a hoarse voice. "My friends won't care if I go back to the resort shirtless."

Kage used Zach's shirt to clean their hands and Zach's belly, wondering how often Zach went home shirtless. Zach lay languidly on the sand, watching Kage's face. He couldn't bring himself to meet Zach's eyes, wondering why he wasn't in a hurry to flee Kage's company.

Kage finally lowered himself onto Zach's relaxed body. Just before they kissed, he saw relief, and something that might have been affection, ghost through Zach's eyes. His mouth quirked upward in humor. His kiss held just as much enthusiasm as it had before they'd come all over each other.

Sitting back again, Kage carefully tucked their cocks back into their jeans. He retrieved his tank top and pulled it on. Climbing to his feet, he held out a hand to help Zach to stand. Kage was pleasantly surprised when Zach stepped into the circle of his arms.

"This has been my best trip to Puerto Vallarta ever," he said against the side of Kage's neck.

Kage chuckled, even as warmth spread through his chest. He ran his hands up and down Zach's back, brushing off the sand. "I certainly never expected to find anyone like you here."

Zach kissed him lightly. "I should go before my friends come looking for me."

"Yeah." Kage was on unfamiliar ground. He'd never had trouble walking away before.

"You'll be okay to get back to your resort?"

Kage snorted. "Yeah, I think I can manage." Still, Zach's concern touched him.

Zach pulled back, smiling self-deprecatingly. "Yeah, I suppose you can."

Kage watched Zach walk back up the beach toward the street, emptiness settling heavily in his stomach. He heard him greet his friends and flag a taxi. Kage shivered with a sudden chill and for the first time, dreaded spending the night alone in his room.

CHAPTER TWO

Kage shifted on his lounge chair. The sun blazed overhead, and it felt good. The heat seeped into his bones and relaxed him, so different from the miserable heat of Iraq. It was also a blessing to wear nothing more than shorts, instead of all the layers of his uniform.

Just when the heat became too intense, a breeze would roll off the ocean and drift across his sweaty skin like a gentle touch. Kage gasped as the memories from two nights ago assailed him. He'd gone back to his room, but sleep had been difficult. Each time he'd closed his eyes, he'd seen Zach's smile, heard his laugh. Kage hadn't showered until the next evening, wanting to keep Zach's scent on his skin. He knew it was ridiculous. Guys like Zach only hooked up with men like Kage; they didn't have relationships with them. Zach probably hadn't given Kage a second thought since he'd left him standing alone on the beach.

Kage wore his sunglasses and had his earbuds in. He wasn't playing music; he just used the buds to keep people from pestering him. It worked to a degree. Some women still insisted on starting conversations. Kage tried not to be rude, but knew he was anyway, giving them abrupt answers and immediately reinserting the earbuds.

If he was honest with himself, he was being an asshole.

Eyes closed, Kage listened to the people around him. They ran through the sand and frolicked in the ocean. The waves roared softly as they rolled up the beach. It was soothing to his raw nerves, even if the sound of the surf conjured thoughts of Zach.

He wondered when the waiter would be back so he could get a fresh beer.

Kage became aware of someone moving close by. It sounded like someone was settling into the lounger that was just a few feet away. Kage's annoyance spiked at the presumption and the intrusion, even as the hair on his arms stood up in irrational reaction to a threat.

"You're not really listening to music, are you?" asked a familiar voice.

Kage's eyes snapped open, and he looked over in surprise to find Zach smiling at him.

"No," he replied, tugging his earbuds out, unable to look away from Zach's gorgeous face. "But it discourages unwanted conversation."

Zach appeared to grow serious. "And is my conversation unwanted?"

"No," Kage replied a little too loudly. "No. You're fine."

"Zach! Hey, Zach," called several people standing around the volleyball net. "Come on and play." Kage recognized the blonde-haired woman who had been dancing with Zach at the bar.

Zach made a distasteful face at them and waved a hand dismissively. He settled down onto the towel-draped lounge chair.

"You don't like volleyball?" asked Kage.

"I just like you better." Zach's full lips curved into a flirtatious smirk.

Kage's mouth went dry, and he wished that waiter would show up. He needed a beer even more now. "What are you doing here?" he finally thought to ask.

"We're staying here." Zach seemed to vibrate with excitement, as if he was sharing an exclusive piece of good news with Kage.

"Here? At this resort?" Kage was sure he'd misunderstood because he just didn't have this kind of good luck.

"Yep. I take it you are, too?" Zach asked excitedly.

"Yeah," Kage answered thoughtfully, still surprised that Zach was engaging him willingly in conversation. "How come we haven't run into each other before now?"

"We haven't been here much," Zach answered. "We went snorkeling one day. Did that zip-line ride yesterday. We decided to just hang on the beach today."

"Sounds like fun," Kage said lamely. He was twice as glad when the waiter showed up to save him from thirst, as well as his own lame conversational skills.

"A Corona and a Pacifico." Zach ordered for them both, as if he did it all the time.

That now-familiar warmth swirled through Kage's belly.

"So, what have you done the last couple of days?" asked Zach.

"You're looking at it." Kage wasn't about to admit to wandering through all the bars in town the night before, hoping in vain to run into Zach.

"Relaxing," Zach said, tipping his head back on the lounge. "Sometimes my friends are so busy being busy they forget to just stop and *be*."

Kage was saved from replying by a volleyball rolling to a stop beside his lounge chair. He tossed it back to Zach's blonde friend when she approached.

"Come on and play with us, Zach," she called, tucking the ball beneath her arm.

"I said no!" Zach yelled back without lifting his head. "Now leave me alone." His annoyance was obviously feigned.

"Your boyfriend can play, too," she called tauntingly.

"He doesn't want to play either," Zach replied tonelessly.

Kage stopped breathing. He'd expected denial. He'd been ready to deny it himself.

"Fine," the woman muttered as she stalked back to the game.

"You didn't want to play, did you?" Zach abruptly lifted his head and asked.

"No," Kage replied with an emphatic shake of his head. Uncharacteristically, he went out on a limb. "I'd rather just sit here and talk to you."

"Good," Zach said happily.

Kage listened and laughed as Zach related anecdotes from his group's excursions the past few days. He seemed closest to his friends Matt and the tall blonde woman named Ashley but spoke of everyone with affection. Kage had no desire to be included in such a large group right now—that would be too much like his platoon back in Iraq—but Kage thought it might be nice to go snorkeling or sailing with just Zach.

There was such animation in Zach's expression as he told his stories. He was quick to smile and his laugh was low and sexy, spreading through Kage's chest like warm caramel. It was easy to respond with smiles, laughter, or questions.

Being with Zach was so easy, so enjoyable, time passed without Kage being aware of it. He was completely relaxed, and it wasn't entirely due to the beer. Even the questions Zach was asking were so innocuous, Kage didn't mind answering. He found he *wanted* to answer.

"Fuck, you are gorgeous," Zach suddenly said with a genuine smile.

Kage choked on his laugh. He hadn't expected that at all. He wasn't gorgeous, was he? He was too hardened, too rough to be attractive to someone as refined and educated as Zach.

"Thank you," he replied quietly. Why couldn't he think of something wittier to say?

"You have such a beautiful smile and the sexiest laugh." Zach shifted on his lounge chair so he was facing Kage more fully.

Kage snorted. "I keep thinking the same thing about you. How is it you're here alone? Why don't you have a boyfriend smart enough not to let you out of his sight?"

Zach laughed in surprise, a warm sound that filled Kage with pleasure. "I can't find one strong enough for me." Even with sunglasses hiding his eyes, his expression seemed meaningful.

"How..." Kage swallowed hard, his pulse hammering in his throat. "Do you mean in bed or out?"

Zach seemed to consider Kage's question. "Both, actually. If they're strong enough for me in bed, they usually aren't man enough for me out of bed."

Kage shook his head, confused. He stopped himself from twisting to face Zach, afraid it might inhibit him from speaking freely.

"I'm a grown man who can manage his own life just fine," Zach elaborated. "I've wounded more than one man's pride by not needing him to take care of me." His expression was shuttered and he glanced around at the other people on the beach.

"You're a college graduate. Why would anyone think you need to be taken care of?" Kage reached for his beer, needing something to do with his hands.

"It's more than that, Kage." Zach sounded almost pleading, like he needed Kage to understand this. "Like the other night when I asked if you'd be okay getting back to your hotel. It was stupid because we both know you don't need to be protected."

"Definitely," he agreed emphatically.

"I don't need protecting either, and you didn't treat me like I did. That was so fucking fantastic." Zach was looking directly at Kage again, it was as unnerving as it was thrilling and Kage was grateful they both wore sunglasses.

Kage shrugged, knowing he was missing some larger point Zach wanted him to understand. "You're at least six feet tall, and you obviously take good care of yourself," he said appreciatively. "Who in their right mind would think you needed protecting?"

Whatever Zach might have answered was lost when two young women began to settle in the set of lounge chairs a couple yards away. Kage's annoyance bordered on anger. Not only did he want to understand what Zach was trying to tell him, he wasn't up to polite social exchanges with women he cared nothing about.

At least Zach didn't appear any happier about the eavesdroppers.

"Hey guys," one of the women greeted as she adjusted her lounge chair.

Zach returned her greeting coolly while Kage gave a half-hearted wave. The women introduced themselves and Zach politely provided their names in return. Kage shifted uncomfortably, the muscles in his back and shoulders tightening.

The woman named Tanya asked, "How long have you guys been here?"

"A few days," answered Zach.

"How do you like it?" she pressed.

Zach looked at Kage when he answered. "The scenery is great. I'm having a blast."

The friend, Bonnie, chimed in. "Are the clubs in town any good?"

"Jalisco's is great," Zach said brightly.

Kage choked on his stifled laughter. Jalisco's was one of the smaller, sleazier bars on the Malicon.

"Awesome," replied Bonnie with a broad smile. "We were thinking of going into town tonight. Do you guys maybe want to come with?"

"That's a generous offer," Zach said solemnly. "But we've decided to stay in tonight." Before either woman could comment or protest, he stood up, faced Kage, and stretched. "I need the men's room," he announced. "I'll be right back, baby."

Kage was rendered speechless when Zach leaned down, grasped his face with both hands, and pressed a hard kiss to his mouth. Kage spanned Zach's ribs with one hand, his skin warm and silky beneath Kage's fingers. Zach pulled back, ending the kiss with a loud smacking sound.

Kage chased the taste with a swipe of his tongue over his own lower lip. His mouth tingled and he couldn't catch his breath.

Both women made sounds of disappointment.

"Oh, that is such a waste," Tanya said.

Kage glanced over to see them both smiling ruefully, without a hint of hostility.

"Not from where I'm standing," Zach called over his shoulder as he crossed the sand to the restrooms.

The women laughed and reluctantly admitted they saw his point.

Kage steeled himself to deal with nosy questions and the women's open admiration of Zach. He was shocked that they both found *him* as attractive as they did Zach. Kage reminded himself they didn't know about his hard edges and his rough manners. He was cynical and distrustful, and people found him hostile. He was lousy at small talk and his casual speech was liberally laced with swear words. Kage knew these women wouldn't like him if they knew about some of the things he'd had to do.

"Hey, Zach!"

Kage's head snapped around to identify the male voice shouting Zach's name. One of his friends held the volleyball and was gesturing Zach over. He was tall, with a thick build that was toned without being overly developed. His face was round and youthful, his dark hair spiked. Zach waved his friend off impatiently.

"Come on and play, man," the friend cajoled. "Your boyfriend can play, too."

Zach's reply was a middle-fingered salute. He smiled at Kage as he approached. "That's Matt. He's pretty much my best friend."

Kage watched Matt casually jog back to the volleyball game, anxiety knotting his stomach. "Your friends aren't going to be pissed off that you're not spending time with them, are they?"

"Fuck no." Zach flopped down onto his lounge chair. "If they demanded excessive amounts of my attention, they wouldn't be my friends."

Kage was getting the idea that Zach had a strong independent streak. He respected and admired that. He was attracted to it, without a doubt.

"Let's go in the surf," Zach said like a delighted child.

Kage liked that idea. He enjoyed the heat, but it was still pretty intense. He also wanted to get close to Zach and he might be able to, if they were in the water.

He stood quickly from his lounge chair and started to follow Zach to the surf. Kage was surprised when Zach turned and held out his hand. Hesitating only a moment, Kage twined their fingers. He smiled when Zach bumped their shoulders together. This kind of easy, open affection was as pleasing to Kage as it was foreign.

The sand was hot beneath their feet, becoming less and less tolerable as they walked. By unspoken agreement, they walked faster. Kage had endured far worse pain, but he could tell Zach was uncomfortable as hell. Even as they picked up their pace, he caught sight of Zach's smile.

Kage broke into a run, using their joined hands to pull Zach after him. He couldn't stop the laughter that burst out of him. He enjoyed Zach's company, especially when he laughed.

They entered the surf with loud splashes. The Sea of Cortez was much warmer than the Pacific Ocean and the surf much less severe. They were in water to their waists when the waves began to break around them. Kage dove under, swimming several strokes before surfacing.

He gave his head a brisk shake and turned back to find Zach standing in the surf, watching him. Kage backstroked several yards farther out before flipping over to dive beneath the water again. He surfaced just inches from Zach.

Kage returned Zach's bright smile. "I thought you wanted to swim."

"That was before I knew you were a fish." Zach laughed.

Kage snorted and had to look away from Zach's face. "The Corps trained me as an advanced diver."

There was no sharp pain in his chest when he admitted that. Kage didn't dread Zach's follow-up questions. It was such a fucking relief.

"They did a damn good job," Zach said admiringly before sliding slowly beneath the waves. He surfaced only a few feet away. "You're very comfortable in the water," he said, pushing his hair from his eyes. "It's sexy."

Kage swam past Zach, their legs only just touching in a slick slide of skin on skin. He wondered what it would be like to pull Zach's body against his own, to press their chests and hips together, and kiss.

"I've also been through jump school," Kage heard himself say. Something about Zach was making it easy for him to talk openly about his service.

"Jump school?"

"Parachuting."

Zach's mouth fell open, and his eyes lit up. "I haven't done that yet!" he exclaimed. "I've always wanted to."

Something pleasant unfurled in Kage's chest. Zach seemed to like to do a lot of the same things he did. Those that Zach hadn't already tried on his own, he at least had an interest in.

They swam farther out, taking their time. When Kage finally stood, the water just reached his shoulders. He glanced around and saw no one near them. Those on the beach weren't paying them any attention at all.

Kage reached out, capturing Zach's wrist and using it to pull him close. Zach eagerly wrapped his legs around Kage's hips. No sooner did Zach have his arms around Kage's neck than their lips met.

It felt like the most natural thing to do.

Zach's body was warm, even in the cooler water. His chest was firm against Kage's. His kiss was eager, his tongue sweeping past Kage's lips, and plunging deep into his mouth. Kage ran his hands up Zach's muscular back, feeling the shift and play of those muscles beneath smooth skin.

Zach moaned. Kage felt it in his mouth and, at the same time, felt Zach's burgeoning erection pushing against his stomach. His own cock was growing harder as Zach rocked his hips against Kage slowly.

When the kiss finally ended, Zach stayed pressed against Kage. "I've wanted to do that since I first saw you lying on that lounge chair." Kage swallowed Zach's sigh.

Kage's heart kicked up in pace. "Me, too." He couldn't help his smile.

"I haven't stopped thinking about you since the night we met." Zach mouthed his way along Kage's jaw.

Kage shuddered. "Me either." He slid his hands down to Zach's firm, rounded ass and squeezed, pulling him closer. It was strangely reassuring that he wasn't the only one with such a strong reaction.

"I've never done that before." Zach's breath was hot as it drifted across Kage's ear. "I've never had a problem walking away with a pleasant memory and not looking back, but I felt so fucking lucky when I saw you again."

"I'm sure you could have easily found some hot guy to roll around in the sand with you." Kage kissed the length of Zach's throat. Jealousy flared hotly at the thought of Zach with anyone else.

"Wouldn't have been the same," he whispered against the corner of Kage's mouth.

Nearby laughter shattered the spell cast around them. Zach pulled back slowly, and Kage reluctantly let him slide from his arms. He swallowed hard past the lump in his throat as he wondered if Zach's words meant just what they sounded like.

They tried body surfing for a while, but the breakers didn't have the height or strength of the Pacific. It was more swimming and floating than anything else. Zach was a strong swimmer, but he was no match for Kage's advanced training.

Between sets of waves, Kage floated, enjoying the heat of the sun on his cool skin. The water muted the sounds around him while amplifying the rush of the tide and sea life. Kage watched the red and yellow light show on the backs of his eyelids. As the water on his chest and face dried, his skin heated, warmth slowly seeping into his bones.

For the first time in over a year, Kage felt both calm and vitally alive.

He gasped when a wave swamped him, chilling his skin, and making him cough. Kage slowly got to his feet, opening his eyes to find Zach smiling at him mischievously.

"Taking your life in your hands, swamping a Marine like that," Kage said with feigned menace.

"I bet once I graduate from the academy, I can hold you off for at least a couple minutes," Zach said, slowly swimming toward shore.

That grabbed Kage's attention and wouldn't let go. "Academy?" He side-stroked next to Zach.

"Yeah. I got hired by the San Diego Sheriff's Department. I start the academy in September." Zach's expression was uncertain. He looked at Kage but never quite met his eyes.

The implications of Zach's softly spoken statement were too great for Kage to process all at once. It explained a lot about his comfort level with Zach. He suddenly understood what it was Zach had been trying to communicate during their earlier conversation.

"Congratulations. That's great." Kage's sudden comprehension was euphoric. He switched to a lazy breaststroke, gliding closer to Zach.

Zach lifted a negligent shoulder that Kage suspected wasn't as casual as it seemed. "It's a start."

"A start to what?" Kage wanted to know everything there was to know about Zach.

"I think I want to go federal eventually." They reached the beach and hauled themselves out of the water. "I could end up just working my way up the ranks of the Sheriff's Department."

Kage chuckled. "So just what is your degree in?"

"Criminal Justice." Zach shook the water from his hair, spraying Kage in the process.

"Ah, yes." Kage half-heartedly dodged the water and laughed.

"I'm thinking of getting a Master's in Administration. I need to get settled at the department, though."

Kage remembered experiencing that same feeling in the weeks before he'd reported to MCRD for Boot Camp. It had been exciting and frightening at the same time. He'd been ready to take on the world and prove himself strong enough and capable enough.

"Your friends know about you, so I assume you're out," he said.

Zach shook more water from his hair as they walked up the sand. "I've been out since high school," he replied. "I know it's going to make things harder, but I'm not going into the closet when I start the academy."

"At least you're not banned entirely from being a cop." Kage knew his bitterness was showing.

"You didn't come out when Don't Ask Don't Tell was repealed?"

"It's not really an issue with the guys in my battalion. I'm a good Marine and that's all the matters."

They reached their lounge chairs, and Kage decided he wanted to finish this conversation at a later time.

When the sun finally began to set and the temperature dipped, Zach and Kage packed up and headed for their rooms.

"Come to dinner with my friends and me," Zach said suddenly.

"I can't," Kage replied before he could stop himself. He ground his teeth together in frustration.

"You can't?" Zach sounded genuinely confused.

Kage sighed. "Loud crowds... they still... I don't quite..."

They reached the elevator to the rooms. "You need more time," Zach said with a knowing nod. His smile was accepting, and Kage thought he might really understand.

A small tendril of relief wound through him. He sighed. "Yeah. Just a little more."

"Well, we're going to be in the bar after dinner if you change your mind or think maybe you could handle the smaller crowd."

"We'll see. I'll think about it." It might be possible if he could move around, keep the teeming crowd in front of him.

The elevator doors opened on the second floor. "Two fifteen," Zach said, pressing a kiss to Kage's mouth. "My room number."

"Three thirty," Kage answered and was rewarded with Zach's brilliant smile.

CHAPTER THREE

He told himself he wasn't checking out the restaurant because he wanted to make Zach happy. It didn't matter anyway; the crowd was too densely packed. Kage broke out in a cold sweat at the idea of being shunted into a corner as strange staff and customers pressed close or bustled by. His skin turned clammy.

He ordered room service and ate in the comfort of his own terrace, watching the last vestiges of sunset. Before, he'd always felt peaceful. Tonight, he was lonely.

The entire front of the bar was glass. Kage stood in the shadows, recon'ing the area of operation. There was a very small dance floor in the back, with the bar on the right. Tables and conversation groups filled the rest of the room. The modest crowd spilled out a door to the left and mingled on the small patio.

With two exits, the patio to retreat to, and enough space to move freely around the room, Kage thought he could do this. He took a deep breath and stepped out of the shadows.

He saw Zach catch sight of him. Kage was pleased with the look of delight that suffused Zach's expression. He was barely in the door before Zach had excused himself from his friends and stepped up to greet him.

"You came," he said, his smile blinding. He ran a hand up Kage's arm and squeezed his bicep firmly.

"Yeah," Kage replied, glancing warily around the room. "I don't know how long I'll be able to stay but…"

"You're here now," Zach finished for him. "Let's get a drink."

Zach's friends were seated in a corner, lounging in a cluster of stuffed chairs and love seats. Kage managed to sit and talk for a while. They were all smart and funny. They seemed to have genuine affection for Zach and were quick to extend it to Kage as well.

It was frustrating when he once again felt the walls closing in on him. He fought it, but when Zach casually laid a hand on his violently bouncing knee, Kage knew he was losing it.

"Want to get some air?" Zach asked quietly, lips pressed to Kage's ear.

Relieved, he nodded sharply and stood. He knew it was rude to leave Zach to make his excuses for him, but he suddenly needed to make it out the door and onto the small patio.

The night air was pleasantly warm and Kage took several deep, steadying breaths.

"Okay?" Zach asked, approaching slowly, his expression cautious.

"I am now, yes," Kage replied, fisting his hands to hide their trembling. It was the truth, though. Now that he was outside, his breathing calmed and his heart slowed.

"I understand if you need to leave." Zach stood several feet away. His face held concern but no signs of the dreaded pity.

"I'm fine now that I'm outside," he said hastily. Kage held out a hand and was pleased when Zach took it immediately, stepping closer just as he'd wanted.

"We can take a walk on the beach," suggested Zach.

Kage's memory flooded with images of the night he and Zach had met. He remembered their shared kisses. He remembered coming in Zach's hand, the feel of Zach climaxing in his. His thoughts must have shown on his face.

Zach chuckled. "That wasn't my intent. However..."

Kage led the way past the pools to the beach. Zach followed, a finger hooked in one of Kage's belt loops. The tide was low, the sound of gently breaking waves carrying to them on the breeze. The air was comfortably cool, filled with the scents of sand and salt.

When they finally stepped outside the reach of the resort's lights, Zach slipped his hand into Kage's. The last of his tension left Kage, carried away on the soothing ocean breeze.

"We're going on one of those party boat tours tomorrow," Zach said after a long while. "We're going to hike to this waterfall that's supposed to be pretty spectacular. You could come if you wanted."

As much as he wanted Zach's company, Kage wasn't ready to be trapped on a boat with strangers, forced to make conversation. There had been a time when he'd have enjoyed that kind of thing. Kage suspected he would again, someday. Just not tomorrow.

Zach correctly interpreted his silence. "It's okay if you can't. I'd like you to, but I understand."

"I must seem pathetic and boring to you." Kage couldn't keep the frustration from his voice.

Zach's dark laughter surprised Kage. "Like I seem spoiled and pampered to you?"

Kage pulled Zach to a stop. "Where the fuck did *that* come from?"

It was hard to see Zach's expression in the dark but he could feel tension rolling off of him.

"You've been back from war less than two weeks," Zach said impatiently. "What you experienced over there has you jumping at shadows and loud noises. Crowds make you uncomfortable, and you can't talk about what you went through." He lifted a hand to Kage's cheek. "Meanwhile, I've been safe at home, having a good time with my friends."

Despite his shock, Kage found his words. "Unless you've been lying to me, in addition to having a good time, you've worked hard to get an education and start yourself a good career."

"You really don't think I'm worthless for staying home and not enlisting?"

"I fight so that you *can* get an education and enjoy your life. If you don't do those things, what do I fight for?"

"Jesus, you're fucking amazing," Zach said, his mouth hovering over Kage's.

He was surprised to find his arms full of a warm and eager Zach. The kiss was wet and aggressive, sending a jolt straight to Kage's cock. The blood rushing in his ears drowned out the sound of the waves lapping at the sand.

Zach was trying to ease them both to the ground. Kage could reverse this if he wanted. He could turn and press Zach down and take his time with him. He liked this, though. Kage's heart slammed in his chest at the idea that Zach wanted *him* this much.

He let himself drop down to the soft sand, not caring that he was wearing his best trousers and an expensive shirt. He'd dressed to impress Zach and it seemed to have worked. Kage pulled Zach down on top of him, licking into his mouth. Zach returned the kiss aggressively, shifting until he straddled Kage's hips.

Kage arched his neck to let Zach mouth his way down the length. He gripped Zach's ass and pulled him in close, vaguely aware of Zach's deft fingers working the buttons of his shirt. When the ends of his shirt parted, Kage shivered. Zach placed open-mouthed kisses along Kage's chest. The ocean breeze chilled the moist skin, making his nipples harden.

"The best part is, you actually *use* this body," Zach said, voice husky, against the heated skin as he licked his way down Kage's abs. "It's not just for looks."

At the feel of Zach's hands opening his fly, Kage ran his fingers through Zach's thick, soft hair. He tried to open his legs to let Zach slide between them, but he couldn't. Zach still sat astride him, keeping him pinned in place.

Kage arched his back and moaned softly when Zach's fingers wrapped around his half-hard cock, pulling it out of his clothing. He knew what this meant, and blood surged into his erection at the thought of Zach's mouth sinking down around him.

"Your dick's just as beautiful as the rest of you." Zach sighed.

Kage huffed a laugh in response. "No one's ever thought anything about me was beautiful before."

"They obviously weren't looking very hard." Zack pushed his mouth down the length of Kage's cock.

Sucking a harsh breath in through his clenched teeth, Kage arched off the sand. He clutched at Zach's shoulders, trying to push his hips up to get himself deeper into that wet heat. Zach's weight on his legs, his hand on Kage's belly, held him in place.

"Oh, fuck." Kage hissed when Zach added his free hand, stroking up and down in time with his mouth. He flexed his hips, pushing against Zach's weight. There was something about the restriction that made the blowjob even hotter. He tried a different tactic, again fisting his hands in Zach's hair.

Zach moaned around him, letting Kage push his head down. Kage shivered as the vibrations rolled through his cock. He glanced down the length of his own tense body. Despite the darkness, Kage could see Zach's sinfully full mouth stretched wide around the width of his dick. Those unusually colored eyes seemed darker with the lack of light, but there was an unmistakable glint of lust and pleasure in them.

Zach sucked hard, pulling back quickly to press his tongue firmly to the underside of Kage's cock. His eyes stayed locked on Kage's, even as Kage urged his head downward again. The head of Kage's dick pressed to the back of Zach's throat and he stopped breathing. When Zach pulled all the way off of Kage's dick, his mouth was swollen and shiny-wet in the dark. He gasped, chest heaving as he caught his breath and watched Kage closely.

"That's so fucking hot," Kage said, low and rough.

"Yeah?" Zach's smile was brilliant. "You smell so fucking good and you taste even better."

Kage didn't know how to respond to that. Instead, he lifted one trembling hand to Zach's chin, cradled it, and skimmed the pad of his thumb along the puffy lower lip. Zach held Kage's gaze as his tongue darted out and licked lightly at Kage's thumb before sucking it into the heat of his mouth.

"Fuck." Kage sighed, his cock twitching painfully.

Releasing Kage's thumb, Zach lowered his head again. He wrapped his fingers around Kage's erection and sucked him down. He tongued at the slit and swirled warm spit around the head. Kage groaned loudly. He watched Zach's head work rhythmically over his groin. The sight, the pressure, the heat were nearly overwhelming.

A shower of sparks ignited at the base of Kage's spine. They scattered through his pelvis and pooled low in his belly. His balls tightened and lifted. Kage panted heavily, his fingers curling convulsively in Zach's hair. The flex of his hips against Zach's restraining weight became erratic as pressure built deep inside, and Kage knew he was close to coming.

"Zach," he said in a harsh whisper, tapping him firmly on the shoulder.

Pulling off with a gasp, Zach stroked Kage with a hand, wet with his own spit. He kissed along the base of Kage's cock. "Come for me, Kage," he said softly. "I wanna feel you come in my hand."

Kage bit back a shout as his climax rolled over him violently. His body convulsed, and his cock pulsed as Zach stroked him fast and hard. Pearly-white ropes of come landed on Kage's belly and chest. Smaller strands ran down his shaft and slid over Zach's fingers. The muscles in his belly and thighs tightened to the point of pain, but Kage didn't care.

When his orgasm released its hold, Kage fell back against the warm sand with a growl. The salty breeze drifted over him, cooling his heated skin. Zach was suddenly above him, kissing him. Kage wrapped his arms around Zach's solid body and held him close.

Zach laughed softly into Kage's mouth.

"What?" Kage asked, confused and wary.

"We're covered in come again and this time, no T-shirt," he replied against Kage's jaw.

Kage joined in the laughter, the humor of their predicament melding with his euphoria. "We'll just have to sneak up to our rooms."

Zach shifted against him, as if trying to stand.

Kage tugged him back down into his lap. "Where are you going?"

"To clean up?" Zach watched him curiously.

"If we're going to all this trouble, we might as well make a real mess." Kage sat up and pulled Zach flush against him. He mouthed the length of Zach's throat.

"You don't have to just because—" Kage stopped Zach's words by kissing him.

"I liked feeling you come against me the other night," he whispered against the hollow of Zach's throat. "I want to feel you again."

He felt Zach's moan more than he heard it. Zach's arms snaked around his shoulders, his hot breath drifted over Kage's temple. When Kage reached between them to unfasten his fly, Zach sucked in his stomach and pressed his hips forward.

Carefully, Kage withdrew Zach's hard cock. He gave a couple of light strokes and smiled when Zach sighed against his hair. Kage pressed his free hand to the small of Zach's back, holding him steady. He squeezed tightly at the head of Zach's erection and felt an answering shudder.

Kage ran his hand the length of Zach's cock. He gave a twist of his wrist and slid his fist down to the base. He took up a fast rhythm, the slide of skin on skin loud, even above the sounds of wind and surf. Zach sat back in Kage's lap, flexing his hips. His grip on Kage's shoulders was almost painful.

Pre-come beaded at the slit and Kage swiped his thumb over it, tearing a low moan from Zach's throat. He watched Zach's expressive face as he jacked him off. Zach's eyes glittered as they stared down into Kage's. His swollen mouth hung open, his lips wet where he'd run his tongue over them. His chest heaved with each harsh breath.

"Are you close?" Kage asked in a whisper, fascinated by the play of sensation across Zach's handsome face.

Zach's eyes grew heavy-lidded, he made a choked sound and trapped his lower lip between his teeth. It was so fucking erotic to Kage, like Zach was fighting his orgasm, struggling to hold it off as long as possible.

"None of that," Kage ordered, his voice rough to his own ears. "Let go and come for me."

Zach gave a small, defiant shake of his head. "Not yet," he gasped.

Kage moved his hand from Zach's back to his cheek, tugging him down for a kiss. He plunged his tongue past Zach's lips and licked deep. Zach groaned as a shudder ran through him.

Pulling back and smiling in triumph, Kage watched Zach start to come. Zach's hips flexed erratically, pushing his cock in and out of Kage's fist. Zach's erection grew a little harder, just before hot strands of come slid down over Kage's fingers.

"Oh, fuck, you bastard," Zach said on a harsh whisper, his eyes slamming shut as he came hard in Kage's hand.

"That's what I wanted," Kage growled against Zach's chin. He stroked Zach's cock until the pulsing stopped and it began to soften. Kage caught him when Zach fell forward, collapsing against him.

They held on to one another for several long moments. Kage was vaguely surprised at how comfortable it was. Zach's breathing slowed, blending with the sound of the gentle ocean waves. The breeze ruffled through Zach's hair and Kage caught the clean scent mingled with salt air, and sex.

Zach finally stirred but Kage was loath to release him. He was surprised when Zach kissed him. It was tender, filled with affection rather than their previous passion. Zach lingered over it and Kage encouraged him. He couldn't remember anyone showing him this kind of care and warmth *after* the sex was over.

"You realize we have to pass by the bar to get to the elevator, right?" Zach asked, smiling against Kage's mouth.

Glancing down at their sandy, disheveled clothes—spotted with come stains—Kage realized their dilemma. Zach's friends would probably see them, and there would be no denying what the two of them had been up to. Kage didn't care. He was proud that Zach had wanted to be with him a second time. As a Marine, he was used to ribald humor, even at his own expense.

But whatever this was between them, Kage didn't want it to be fodder for off-color jokes.

He remembered the narrow path he'd found that wound around the far side of the resort's main restaurant. "Come on," he said, with a gentle swat to Zach's ass. "I have an idea."

They climbed to their feet, helping each other straighten and dust off their clothes. Neither of them looked like they'd been doing anything other than what they had been: getting each other off.

Kage took Zach's hand, leading him down the beach and through the quiet grounds of the resort. The thumping sound of music from the bar drifted to them, as did loud and raucous conversation and laughter. When they reached the point in the stone path that would lead them between the main restaurant and the bar, Kage took the smaller fork that bent to the right.

Circling around the restaurant and leading them to a little-used corridor, Kage navigated the alternate path. He smiled at Zach in triumph when they reached the bank of elevators, encountering no one else along the way.

"Cross your fingers there's no one in the elevator," Zach said quietly, the corner of his mouth lifting slightly and his eyes shining with humor.

"Almost home free," Kage replied, placing a kiss just below Zach's ear. He imagined Zach leaned into him.

Luck was with them; the elevator car was empty. They rode to the second floor, standing shoulder to shoulder. When the doors opened, Kage followed Zach.

"Are you walking me to my door?" Zach asked, smiling hesitantly.

"I thought I would, yes." Kage buried his fists in his trouser pockets, feeling suddenly awkward.

"I'm not a girl." Zach's smile faded, his expression darkened. He turned and walked quickly down the corridor. "You don't need to make sure I get to my room safely."

Their conversation from earlier that day came back to Kage in a rush. "I know you're not a girl. I'm not worried for your safety." He couldn't bring himself to finish his explanation.

"You enjoy my company so much you just want to prolong our time together," Zach said over his shoulder, sarcasm lacing every word.

Kage's face flushed, and he glanced away from Zach's flashing green eyes. Zach slowed until he matched Kage's stride. He made himself look at Zach again and found him watching him closely, his expression surprised and wary.

"Good," Zach finally said quietly. "I feel the same way."

Kage's knotted stomach eased. He swallowed hard. They reached Zach's door, but he didn't seem in a hurry to go inside. Kage contemplated dragging Zach back to his own room and spending the entire night memorizing his body. He just wasn't sure he was ready for that level of intimacy yet.

"I'll keep an eye out for you when we get back tomorrow," Zach said, unlocking his door but not stepping in. "Maybe you can try coming to dinner with us."

"We'll see." Kage didn't have high hopes for that. Instead, he leaned in and captured Zach's mouth for a goodnight kiss. He tried to make it hot and sensual. He'd never felt so awkward and unskilled.

To his surprise, Zach leaned into him, opening his mouth readily, and meeting his tongue eagerly. He cradled Zach's head gently, licking into his mouth slowly and languidly. Zach's breathing sped up, become a harsh. Kage's own breathing was the same.

He pulled back slowly, reluctantly. "Have fun tomorrow," he whispered, placing another quick kiss on Zach's wet lips. "See you soon." He didn't look back as he headed for the elevator. Inside his room, Kage paced, knowing he wouldn't be able to sleep. He took a beer out of the small fridge and stepped out onto the terrace. The sounds of the revelry from the bar drifted up to him. Kage's knee bounced violently. Despite the alcohol, he couldn't relax and settle down. Instead of feeling like a safe haven, Kage's room felt isolated and lonely. Maybe he should have brought Zach back here after all.

CHAPTER FOUR

Two days later, Kage walked past the pools on his way to the beach. It was early morning and he hadn't seen Zach at all since their goodnight kiss. Zach and his friends had probably returned from their party cruise and headed to the Malicon to keep things going. Kage didn't expect to see Zach before noon, if at all.

"Hey!" said a voice near his ear as two arms came around him, pinning him.

Adrenaline spiked through Kage's body. He lifted his arms and stepped sideways to break the hold of his attacker. Even as he made his evasive moves, something inside Kage knew there was no threat. He turned to see Zach backing away, hands up, palms out as if in surrender. "My bad," he said, expression contrite. "I was excited to see you, and I didn't think."

Kage was deeply chagrined. He took a deep breath and rolled his shoulders to relax the tension. His heart still slammed against his ribs, even as he tried to calm down. Kage knew that, three weeks ago, he might have hurt Zach before he'd realized the threat wasn't real.

"You startled me," he said, clearing his throat. "I didn't expect to see you until much later."

"I went to bed early," Zach replied, taking a hesitant step toward Kage. "Too much sun and alcohol yesterday," he said sheepishly.

Kage nodded and turned back toward the beach. "What are your plans for today?" He knew what he hoped Zach's plans were.

"We're hanging out at the pool." Zach gestured toward the tables and lounge chairs his friends had commandeered. They'd claimed prime real estate in front of the Ping-Pong tables next to one of the bars. "You'll join us, won't you?"

Kage liked Zach's friends and, out in the open, he shouldn't have trouble with the crowd. It was probably a good sign that he didn't want to isolate himself anymore. "Yeah, that'd be fun."

Zach's smile was blinding and Kage's heart did something funny in his chest.

By mid-morning, the heat was near-sweltering. The sunlight glinted brightly off the pools and they sparkled beautifully. As a concession to the early hour—but with no desire to delay the party—the group ordered mimosas and screwdrivers instead of beer. They were humoring themselves and everyone knew it.

Kage was sweating as the sun beat down on him, heat seeping through his muscles and into his bones. He felt buzzed and languorous. He hadn't been this relaxed since before his deployment.

He turned to Zach, sprawled on the lounge chair next to him and looking too enticing for the public venue. "I'm going for a swim to cool off."

"I'll come, too," Zach said eagerly, taking off his shades and jumping to his feet.

Kage dove into the crystal clear water, shocked by the cold until the chill felt good. He kicked halfway across the pool before he surfaced. Zach came up a few feet away.

"Hey, I wanna show you something," Zach said with a teasing smile. He side-stroked toward the narrow connection between the upper and lower pools.

Kage followed Zach when he veered to the side, swimming beneath a wooden footbridge. They emerged in a shadowed lagoon that Kage hadn't known existed. As he stood, glancing around and admiring the secluded beauty of the spot, Zach came up from behind and pressed against him.

Chuckling, Kage turned to face him. The slick feel of their wet skin touching and gliding was highly erotic. Zach's eyes were heavy-lidded, his lips parted and moist as he stared blatantly at Kage's mouth.

Holding still, Kage sighed in satisfaction when Zach leaned in and kissed him.

"I missed you yesterday," Zach said against his lips.

"Me too," he replied, swiping his tongue over Zach's delectable lower lip.

They kissed again, Zach's breathing speed up, matching Kage. He wrapped his arms around Zach and felt his heart pounding through his chest.

Zach started to pull back but Kage held on, not wanting to let him go. That desire frightened him a little. He should think about what this all meant.

"We should get back before my friends come looking for us," Zach sighed.

"Do they really care?" Kage kissed the length of Zach's throat.

"They'll come looking just 'cause they think they can embarrass us." He chuckled.

"Later on, we should go somewhere private."

Zach stilled in Kage's arms, but he didn't tense and he didn't pull away. Zach buried his face in the join of Kage's shoulder and neck and quietly said, "Yeah, let's do that."

Slowly, they swam back to Zach's friends. The group welcomed them with catcalls and promises to track them down if they disappeared again. Kage lifted himself onto the pool deck, smiling, taking the fresh beer Ashley handed him.

"So, it's late enough now, no more need to camouflage the alcohol?" He smiled at her, lifting the bottle to his lips.

"Yeah. Well, you know how it is; it's always twelve o'clock somewhere." Ashley returned his smile, nudging him with her shoulder.

While they'd been gone, another group of people had invaded the pool. Everyone was mingling and Kage was introduced to several young, attractive men and women. Despite the crowd and the noise, he was calm. Kage was even enjoying himself.

"Are you any good at Ping-Pong?" Zach asked.

Kage snorted. "Sometimes during lockdown on base, the Ping-Pong table is the only distraction."

"Good," Zach replied smugly. "Let's play."

They did a hell of a lot more drinking and bullshitting, than playing Ping-Pong. The crowd was a major distraction, shouting more harassment than encouragement. Neither Kage nor Zach was drunk, but their motor skills were undoubtedly impaired.

"Do you guys know how to play doubles?"

Kage turned, surprised to find an extremely hot guy standing just a few feet away. He had the look of a jock, with a heavily-muscled upper body and legs, and sharply-cut abdominal muscles. With Zach standing just a few feet away, tan skin slick with sweat and smiling suggestively, Kage barely gave the jock a second look.

Zach shrugged at Kage, passively agreeing to the game. Kage would have moved to Zach's side of the table when the new pair instead split up. The blond woman teamed up with Zach, and the jock took his position next to Kage.

The game was fun but the jock, Kevin, was a better player than his friend Megan. They beat her and Zach so badly, game after game, that things dissolved into little more than swinging paddles and loud laughter. The first few times Kevin touched Kage, he had to hide his startled reaction before shrugging him off. Eventually, Kage got his reactions under control. There was no threat here. Kevin was simply being friendly. Besides, they were playing a game. Some physical contact was expected and unavoidable.

Finally, Megan surrendered. She tossed down her paddle and threw up her hands. Kevin went with her to the bar to help carry back their drink order.

Kage looked up, surprised to find Zach standing directly in front of him, so close he could feel the heat radiating off his skin. Zach's sunglasses prevented Kage from seeing his eyes, but he was standing too close for his intent to be casual. Kage's breath caught in his chest.

"God, I want to kiss you so fucking much right now," Zach said in a low and dangerous voice.

Kage's cock responded to Zach's tone with a twitch. "I wish you could, but we *are* in public." The crowd seemed tolerant, and they might have gotten away with it, but Kage didn't want to take the chance.

"I almost don't care." Zach splayed a hand on Kage's side, just above the waist of his shorts. "Just so Kevin will back the fuck off."

Kage barked a surprised laugh, glancing with disbelief in Kevin's direction. "We're just playing drunken Ping-Pong!"

"Megan doesn't know how to play Ping-Pong. She was being a good friend and helping Kevin get close to you."

Kage covered Zach's hand where it rested against his ribs. Kage was too coarse and rough for an all-American like Kevin. Then again, Zach should be finding Kage too unrefined for his tastes. "You're more his type than I am." He wished his words didn't ring so true. "But is *he* more *your* type than I am?"

Kage stared hard at Zach, taking in the tense lines of his body. He wished he could see Zach's eyes behind the sunglasses. It seemed like Kage's answer mattered to him and that mattered to Kage. "I'm sorry. Who were we talking about?" he asked with feigned confusion. "I was too busy staring at the luscious mouth I'm going to spend all night kissing."

Zach's answering smile had something warm and comfortable spreading through Kage's belly. "Just be sure you let him down gently. He seems like a nice guy," Zach said magnanimously.

Megan and Kevin returned with the drinks, and Zach withdrew his hand, leaving Kage feeling bereft. He enjoyed Zach's touch and that streak of jealousy and possessiveness he'd just witnessed stirred something primal in him.

Kage became hyperaware of Kevin's proximity. Whether sitting in the lounge chairs beside the pool or at the swim-up bar, Kevin was never more than a few feet from Kage. Zach was frequently just out of Kage's reach, watching him, a knowing smile dancing across his lips. He finally admitted to himself that Zach was right: not only was Kevin always close by, he also touched Kage a lot.

It was all casual, but Kevin was touching Kage more than anyone else did, even more than Zach. He considered telling the guy to keep his hands to himself, but he remembered Zach's request that Kage let him down easy.

By late afternoon it was still blisteringly hot. Kage sat on the foot of a lounge chair surrounded by a cluster of Zach's friends. He noticed Ashley's beer was empty and offered to get her another. As he stood, Zach skimmed his palm along the small of Kage's back.

"That's nice of you," Zach said quietly, making Kage's heart do that strange thing that felt vaguely like a flutter. Kage was a Marine. His heart didn't flutter.

Kage was at the bar waiting for their drinks when Matt came to stand next to him.

"I know you're supposed to be some killer Marine and all," Matt said without preamble. "But if you hurt Zach, I will find a way to fuck you up."

That got Kage's attention. He turned to give Matt his full attention. "Don't think we don't all see how that brainless quarterback has had his hands all over you," Matt continued. "You're not giving him the time of day, and Zach seems okay with it, so we're letting it slide for now. But if you ditch Zach to go "walk on the beach" with that other guy, no amount of fancy military training will matter."

The ferocity of Matt's loyalty to Zach struck a familiar chord in Kage. The kid might make a decent Marine, especially with his direct, plain-spoken manner. Kage knew exactly how to handle this situation.

He paid for the drinks and turned to face Matt. "Zach is more than capable of taking care of himself. He doesn't need you to protect him. But I respect your loyalty to him, so I'll share some intel with you. I made it clear to Zach that I have no interest in Kevin, and Zach asked me not to make a scene. That's the only reason I haven't already put my fist through the guy's pushy face."

Matt laughed and shook his head, as if in disbelief. "You're right. Zach *can* take care of himself. It's just... he's different around you."

Kage's stomach plummeted. "Different?"

Matt grew serious again. "It's about more than just his dick this time."

"Oh," Kage replied lamely. "Good." Smug satisfaction rolled through him.

Matt helped Kage carry the drinks. "If Zach won't let you punch the guy, maybe he'll let me," he said, just before they were back in earshot.

Kage dove into the pool to cool off, swimming leisurely toward the upper pool. When he pressed his back against the side, bracing his arms on the coping, he was surprised to see Kevin swimming toward him. Annoyance flared in Kage. This guy just could not take a hint.

"Hey," Kevin greeted, swimming blatantly into Kage's personal space.

Kage let out an irritated sigh. "You know, Kevin, you're a nice guy. But I've made it as clear as I can, without being rude, that I'm not interested."

Kevin's expression was doubtful. "Are you really with Zach? 'Cause it's hard to tell."

Kage frowned, his annoyance flaring. "Even if I wasn't, I don't like being pushed."

Kevin drew a breath and started to swim even closer.

Kage's annoyance swiftly turned to anger. He pressed two fingers into Kevin's chest to stop his forward movement. "You need to learn to take no for an answer."

Ignoring Kevin's surprised expression, Kage pushed off from the wall and swam back to the group. They were sitting on the edge of the pool, feet in the water. As he approached, Matt slid over to make room between himself and Zach.

Kage pressed his hands to the deck and gave one push with his arms. He came out of the water and seated himself right next to Zach, their hips and thighs touching.

"Have a nice swim?" Zach asked, smiling.

"No. It was interrupted by someone who wasn't you," Kage replied, leaning in to press a hard kiss to Zach's mouth. He caught the look of surprise on Zach's face just before he closed his eyes. Kage let it linger. He didn't care who saw. He knew Kevin was watching and that's all that mattered.

When he pulled back, Zach was blushing. "Wha— wha— what was that for?" he stuttered, sounding nervous.

Kage glanced around and didn't see anyone outside of their group paying attention.

"You and I have plans for tonight, don't we?" asked Kage.

"Yes," Zach answered hastily.

"Good," Kage said emphatically. "Now everyone knows I have no interest in changing those plans."

Zach's blush deepened. "Oh." He ran his tongue over his lower lip as if chasing Kage's taste. Kage tracked the movement.

His mouth suddenly dry, Kage took a long drink of his beer. He lowered the bottle to find Matt extending his own bottle. Kage tapped the neck of his bottle against Matt's.

"Well played, my friend," Matt said with a spiteful smile. "And bonus points for making Zach blush," he added quietly. "Can't remember the last time *that* happened."

Kage wondered what it meant that both he and Zach were reacting to each other in ways they normally didn't react to anyone. He suddenly dreaded the time they would all have to return to the real world.

CHAPTER FIVE

Kage managed to make it through dinner with Zach and his friends by carefully placing himself in a corner, out of the flow of foot traffic. He'd even managed to enjoy himself a little.

More than anything else, he'd enjoyed watching Zach have a good time. Kage realized there was little he wouldn't do to see Zach smile.

After the meal, Kage accepted hugs from Ashley and Matt.

"You guys have a safe trip home," he told them.

"I hope we see you again," said Ashley, tugging him down so she could kiss his cheek.

"Thank you," Kage replied. He wanted to. He wanted to see them all again once they were home, which was surprising as hell.

Zach's friends headed out front to catch a taxi to the Malicon for one last night of partying in Mexico. Kage and Zach headed for the elevator for the short ride to Kage's room.

As Kage closed and locked the door, his mouth went dry as dust. He wiped his sweaty palms on his jeans. Just thinking about Zach being here made his cock ache. Kage took two beers out of the small fridge and joined Zach on the terrace.

They stood together at the railing, nearly touching, but not quite. The ocean breeze was strong, ruffling Zach's dark hair. Kage turned his face into it and inhaled the scent of salt. Things were going to be different when Zach left tomorrow. Kage knew his own life would never be the same.

He finished his beer, contemplating getting another. His mouth was still so fucking dry. Kage decided against more alcohol. He couldn't chance impairing his performance. Kage's heart raced and he realized he'd been so lost in his own thoughts, he hadn't noticed Zach's uncharacteristic silence.

"Need another beer?" he asked, the roughness of his voice surprising him.

"No, thank you," Zach said quickly. He seemed reluctant to meet Kage's eyes.

"Are you having second thoughts?" Kage's stomach made a queasy roll.

"No," Zach said hastily. He sighed heavily. "I just... I don't want... fuck." He ran an agitated hand through his hair.

Zach's nervousness confused the hell out of Kage. Suddenly, a thought struck him and their conversation that first day on the beach, took on new meaning. Zach needed to let go but didn't want to appear weak.

Kage reached for Zach, grasping his face with both hands and kissing him hard. He pushed his tongue past Zach's parted lips, licking into his mouth aggressively. Zach fisted his hands in Kage's shirt. He changed the angle of the kiss as Zach stepped into him, pressing their hips together firmly. Zach's erection was growing against Kage's own hardening cock.

Pulling back on a gasp, Kage pressed his lips to Zach's sweaty temple. "Just because I want to have you naked beneath me, to have my cock deep inside your ass, doesn't mean I want you weak and submissive, tomorrow." Zach shuddered, releasing a shaky breath, his grip on Kage's shirt tightening. "Will you let me fuck you?" Kage asked in a whisper. "Please?"

"Yes," Zach moaned. The lingering tension seemed to flee his body and Kage silently celebrated.

Pulling back, he grabbed the front of Zach's shirt, using it pull him off the terrace and back into the room. He slid the door shut. "I want you to make as much noise as you want to, without the entire hotel hearing."

Zach flushed at Kage's words. His tongue darted out to wet his lower lip.

Kage pushed Zach through the bedroom door. He unbuttoned his own shirt, sliding it off his shoulders, letting it fall negligently to the floor. When Zach's hands moved to his own top button, Kage stopped him.

"No," he said firmly, holding Zach's gaze. "I'm going to do that."

Zach's hands fell to his sides, and he swallowed hard. Stepping right into Zach's space, Kage nosed at his temple, breathing in the scents of sweat and cologne. Slowly, he unfastened the buttons of Zach's shirt, slid it slowly off his shoulders, down his arms, finally tossing it aside.

Kage skimmed his hands down Zach's chest and belly. His skin was warm, tanned, and silky under Kage's palms. The muscles of his stomach flexed and contracted when Kage dragged his fingertips along the sharp planes.

"Touch me if you want to," Kage told him.

Zach's arms went around Kage like he'd been waiting for permission. He caressed Kage's back, his touch firm and sure. Kage pressed an open-mouthed kiss to Zach's collarbone and heard him moan softly. Zach brought his hands around and stroked down Kage's chest, flicking this thumbs over Kage's nipples.

Kage shuddered, moaning into Zach's neck.

"You're so fucking strong," Zach murmured.

"Do you want that?" Kage asked, lifting Zach's face for a kiss. "You want me to use my strength on you?"

"God, yes," Zach growled against his jaw.

Lifting his hands to Zach's shoulders, Kage urged him to sit at the foot of the bed. He pushed Zach's knees apart, kneeling between them. With one hand, he gripped Zach's chin. "I'm going to suck you off. Then I'm going to spread you out, face down on my bed, and I'm going to fuck you."

Zach exhaled harshly like he'd been gut-punched. His pupils were blown wide with desire, and he breathed heavily through parted lips. It was the hottest thing Kage had ever seen, and it amazed him that he could bring Zach to this point.

Kage opened Zach's belt and unzipped his fly. He tugged Zach's jeans down over his hips and legs, while Zach shifted around as he tried to help. Pulling the clothes, shoes and all, off of Zach's body, he tossed everything aside. Kage sat back on his heels to admire in the light, what he'd only caught glimpses of in darkness.

Zach was gorgeous. His bronze skin was covered in a light sheen of sweat. His dark nipples were hard, and his beautiful cock pressed against his belly, dusky red and heavily veined. Kage's mouth watered. Zach's erection twitched and a bead of pre-come formed at the slit.

Kage pressed his palm to the center of Zach's chest, giving him a firm push. "Lay back," he ordered. Zach reclined onto his elbows and Kage draped his forearm over Zach's hips. When he pressed Zach's hips into the bed, restraining him, Zach's eyelids fluttered and he gasped softly.

Kage smiled up at him just before he lowered his head. He wrapped his other hand around the base of Zach's cock, holding him steady. Kage lapped at the bead of pre-come on the head of Zach's dick.

"Oh, my God," Zach sighed.

Kage slid his lips over the width of Zach's dick, pressing his tongue flat to the underside of the shaft. He pushed himself down, getting Zach as close to the back of his throat as he could. Pulling back, Kage hollowed his cheeks and sucked hard, keeping his lips tight around his teeth. He dragged his hand up, following his mouth, until he could tongue at Zach's slit again.

Kage swallowed Zach's length, gripping tight with his fist. He pressed his tongue firmly to the fat vein on the underside of Zach's cock. He found a slow rhythm that dragged harsh breaths and low moans from Zach. Kage kept his arm across Zach's hips, restricting his reflexive lift. Zach pushed against Kage, grunting in frustration, only to give a dirty moan a moment later.

Speeding up his rhythm, Kage gave his wrist a couple of quick twists. Zach's cock was sloppy with spit and Kage's palms slid easily over the slick skin. Zach swore, falling back onto the bed all the way. He ran a hand over Kage's hair, fisting the other in the bed-clothes.

Kage pulled off of Zach's cock, smiling at his sound of protest. He hooked his hands behind Zach's knees and lifted, opening him up and placing his feet flat on the mattress. Kage sucked on two of his own fingers just before he slid his mouth back down Zach's shaft.

Resuming his fast rhythm, Kage pushed his two spit-slick fingers into Zach's tight hole. Zach arched his back, clutching at Kage's head with both hands.

"Oh, fuck," he cried, his hips thrusting upward and pushing his erection further into Kage's mouth.

Kage took it easily, sliding his fingers in and out of Zach's heat in time with the motion of his mouth. Zach trembled, his inner muscles clenching tight. Kage stilled his fingers and crooked one, just a little. He searched carefully until he found the right spot.

Zach shouted wordlessly, his shoulders lifting off the bed convulsively. He fell back down as Kage moved his fingers in time with his mouth. Zach's chest heaved with his every harsh breath and Kage pressed his fingers upward again.

"Kage," Zach cried, his tone desperate. His fingers tightened around Kage's head. "Kage, please. I don't want to come like this."

Kage pulled off of Zach's straining cock and slid his fingers free. Carefully, he lowered one of Zach's feet to the floor and straddled that leg. He leaned over Zach, lips hovering just over his mouth, and licked at his bitten lower lip. "I'm going to make you come just to take the edge off. Then we'll go again, together, with me inside of you."

"Oh, fuck," Zach moaned shakily.

Kage pushed his fingers back into Zach's hole, using his other hand to stroke his shaft. He kept his face just above Zach's, watching every sensation, every emotion that crossed it. Kage pushed his fingers upward into Zach's gland and watched his orgasm roll over him.

Zach's sex flush deepened, his eyes slammed shut. His neck arched, his mouth falling open in a silent cry of pleasure. His body tightened even more around Kage's fingers, his hips rocking up and down erratically. He twisted one hand in the bedclothes, flexing the fingers of his other hand against the back of Kage's head.

When the first splash of hot come landed on Zach's belly, Kage crooned encouragement. He stroked

Zach's hard, pulsing cock as strand after strand of opalescent come coated his hand, and Zach's sweaty skin. Zach cried out between harsh, gasping breaths. When he opened his eyes and his gaze locked unerringly with Kage's, it felt like time stopped.

Zach fell back against the bed, his spent cock softening in Kage's hand. Carefully, he released Zach, lowering his head for a kiss. Zach gasped into his mouth when Kage slid his fingers from his ass.

Pulling back, Kage looked into Zach's flushed face. He looked absolutely wrecked, and Kage was amazed that he'd been the one to cause it.

"I'll be right back," he whispered against Zach's mouth.

Ducking into the bathroom, Kage wet a cloth with warm water and grabbed up several hand towels. Returning to the bedroom, Kage quickly cleaned Zach's belly and chest of drying come. Satisfied with his efforts, Kage stood, quickly stripping off the rest of his own clothing. He knew he was clumsy, but the sight of a languid Zach, collapsed on the bed, made his cock ache painfully.

"Come on, up you go," Kage encouraged, helping Zach up the bed. He urged him to lie face down, arms curled around a single pillow. Kage spread Zach's thighs and knelt between them. Zach watched him carefully from over his shoulder. Kage's heart swelled at the sight of Zach spread out naked just for him. Zach arched up into his hands as Kage skimmed them over his smooth skin. He slid his palms over Zach's ass, admiring how firm and round it was.

Zach was so beautiful, it was nearly painful. Kage half expected to wake up any moment to discover this was all just a dream.

"Kage?" Zach's soft voice dragged Kage from his thoughts. "Is something wrong?" His expression was wary.

Kage smiled at him ruefully. "Not a thing."

He lowered himself over Zach's body, Zach arching up into him. Pressing his nose just below Zach's ear, Kage inhaled. The scent of Zach's shampoo mingled with soap and sweat. There was just a hint of musky cologne that Kage really enjoyed. He flicked his tongue along the shell of Zach's ear, nipped at the lobe, and felt Zach moan and shiver beneath him.

Kage skimmed his hands over Zach's naked back. "You smell so good," he whispered, biting lightly on Zach's earlobe.

Zach gasped, his hips pushing upward into Kage's.

"You taste good, too," Kage said, just before biting the straining tendon in the back of Zach's neck. He soothed the spot with his tongue. Beneath him, Zach groaned low in his throat.

Shifting lower, Kage dragged the flat of his tongue along the top of Zach's spine to the base of his neck. Zach's hands fisted in the bed clothes, and he began to writhe. Kage moved lower still, licking at the sweat that collected along Zach's spine, nipping gently at the smooth skin over his ribs.

Kage reached Zach's hips, felt him grinding into the bed beneath them. He spanned Zach's narrow waist with both hands and stilled him. Kage pressed his thumbs into the enticing dimples at the swell of Zach's ass. Zach moaned when Kage lowered his head and licked at each spot.

"You sure are taking your time," Zach said with a breathy laugh.

Kage's chest tightened. "You're not enjoying yourself?"

"No! I mean, yes!" Zach made a frustrated sound. "I just don't know what you're thinking about."

The tightness in Kage's chest eased. He smiled against the skin of Zach's lower back. "I'm thinking about all the things I want to do to your gorgeous body."

Zach snorted, but his smile looked pleased. "You've got a better body than I do."

The compliment warmed Kage. Not sure how to respond, he nipped at one of Zach's ass cheeks. Zach gasped, then chuckled in response.

Sliding down between Zach's thighs, Kage flicked the tip of his tongue at the very top of the cleft of his ass. Zach jolted, huffing an embarrassed laugh. Kage adjusted his grip and spread Zach's ass cheeks.

"Oh, fuck," Zach sighed harshly. He tucked the pillow beneath his head and chest, gripping it tightly with both fists.

"Okay?" Kage asked, blowing a puff of air across Zach's hole, watching it clench reflexively.

"Yeah," Zach replied in a rough voice, lifting his hips encouragingly. Kage ran the tip of his tongue from Zach's ball sac, to the base of his spine and heard Zach moan. He did the same with the flat of his tongue, and Zach pushed back into him. Kage spread Zach's ass wider, swirling his tongue around the tight opening of his hole.

Dipping lower, Kage mouthed at Zach's heavy sac. Zach groaned and swore, his hips pumping without rhythm. Kage focused on Zach's hole, pushing his tongue in, tasting musk and tang. The way Zach moved, the sounds he made, fired Kage's blood. He licked into Zach's body, spreading his ass wider and wider. Zach's hole relaxed, and Kage flicked his tongue deeper. His own cock ached painfully. Kage ground his hips into the bed and the friction was almost unbearable.

Rising to his knees, Kage licked the length of Zach's spine and felt him shiver. He lowered himself over Zach's body, and it was like his skin was on fire. He smoothed Zach's sweat-damp hair back from his forehead and pressed his lips to Zach's ear.

"I'm going to get you ready," he whispered.

"I don't need much." Zach lifted his hips.

Kage shushed him, placing open-mouthed kisses along Zach's jaw. Zach tilted his head back, seeking Kage's lips. Kage kissed Zach, licking deep into his mouth. They both breathed heavily, the sound loud in the quiet room.

Reaching into the drawer of the bedside table, Kage retrieved a small lube bottle and a condom. Carefully, he covered two of his fingers with the cool gel. Kage steadied Zach with a hand on his hip, sliding his fingers into Zach's ass. If it was possible, Zach was even hotter than he had been earlier. His body opened easily for Kage's fingers.

Twisting his wrist, Kage spread the slick inside Zach's tight channel. He slid his fingers out, pushing them back in to the last knuckles. Zach pushed back against him, groaning. Picking up the lube bottle again, Kage eased his fingers out of Zach's hole.

"I'm good, I'm ready," Zach gasped, looking over his shoulder as Kage added lube to his fingers.

"Not as ready as I want you to be," replied Kage, pushing two slick fingers back into Zach's ass.

Zach groaned like he was in pain and Kage almost stopped moving. "You're gonna fucking kill me."

Kage laughed softly. He worked his fingers in Zach's hole, ensuring a slick glide for his cock. He pressed his fingertips downward into that firm gland he found easily now.

"Oh, fuck," Zach cried. He clutched at the pillow beneath him. "Kage." His harsh whisper sounded like a plea.

Kage kissed the base of Zach's spine. "I've got you."

Withdrawing his fingers again, Kage lubed three of them this time. He pushed his fingers into Zach's clenching hole, and it was like Zach's body was drawing him in. He twisted his fingers, massaging Zach's gland. Zach shuddered violently.

"Oh, God!" Zach pleaded. "Now, please, Kage. I need you."

Zach's desperation hit Kage like a body blow. Blood surged into his own cock, overwhelming him with the need to be inside of Zach. He eased his fingers from Zach's hole and reached for the condom. Struggling with trembling fingers, Kage rolled the condom onto his own erection. "Hold yourself open for me," he said, trying to remember to breathe.

Zach pushed the pillow aside and drew up one knee. He hooked his arm behind his knee and pulled his leg higher, spreading his ass wide. Kage lay himself down on top of Zach, craving his heat.

"You're so fucking gorgeous," Kage breathed against the back of Zach's neck. His cock ached, and he was desperate to push himself into Zach's heat.

Reaching between their bodies, Kage lined himself up with Zach's hole and flexed his hips. He pushed inward, slipping into Zach's body. He groaned at the feel of Zach surrounding him, taking him in.

Zach fisted his free hand in the bedclothes. He moaned loudly, lifting his hips as if to get more of Kage's cock inside. Kage braced his hands on either side of Zach and thrust his hips hard. He slid deep into Zach's ass.

"Kage!" Zach's cry was a desperate plea.

Kage held himself still, covering Zach's hand with his own, and twined their fingers. He buried his face in Zach's hair, breathing him in. Beneath him, Zach's chest heaved with every breath.

"Are you okay?" Kage asked, shocked at the quaver in his own voice.

"Yeah," Zach gasped. "Just..."

"I've got you," he whispered into Zach's hair, again smoothing back his sweaty bangs.

Kage started a steady rhythm, rocking his hips against Zach's ass, sliding his cock in and out of him. Zach lay beneath him, rocking up into each thrust. He breathed heavily between low groans and gasps. Kage ran a hand down Zach's back, feeling gooseflesh rise on his skin. Their twined fingers gripped tight.

Zach's brilliant eyes were open but his look was distant and unseeing. His brow was furrowed as if he was in pain. A chill of fear raced down Kage's spine.

"Am I hurting you?" Kage asked, nuzzling Zach's ear.

"No! Fuck no." Zach's response was emphatic and his body bowed upward into Kage's.

When Zach lifted his face and looked over his shoulder, Kage eagerly gave him the kiss he sought. Relief swept through him as he realized Zach's frown was a sign of his pleasure.

Breaking the kiss, Kage rose up onto his knees. "Kneel up with me," he urged, helping Zach to move with him so that his cock didn't slip free.

Kage eased Zach to straddle his hips, his erection pushing deep inside of him. Zach cried out. His hands reached back to grip Kage's hips. He arched his back, his head falling against Kage's shoulder.

Reaching back, Kage twined his fingers with Zach's, bringing their hands around to rest on Zach's thighs. He licked the length of Zach's neck before nipping lightly at a straining tendon. Zach rocked slowly in Kage's lap, grinding down onto his cock.

Kage looked down the length of Zach's body, seeing he was hard again. Zach's cock bounced freely with his movements. It was a dusky red and weeping freely from the slit.

"Get yourself off for me," Kage said against Zach's shoulder. "I want to feel you around me when you come." He moved their joined hands toward Zach's erection.

Zach wrapped his hand around his own cock and tugged slowly a few times. He adjusted his grip and fell into a fast, steady rhythm. Zach's eyes fell shut and his mouth hung open as he jacked himself. The rough sound of skin on skin filled the room as Zach's hand moved in a blur. His hips rocked a little in Kage's lap, his inner muscles clenching Kage's cock tight.

Kage kept his face pressed to the crook of Zach's neck. He watched the blood-red head of Zach's erection disappear over and over into his fist. He pushed his own hips upward in time with Zach's rhythm, fucking his ass as Zach jacked himself, riding Kage's cock.

"I'm gonna come," Zach gasped. "I'm gonna come again."

"Good, that's what I want," Kage whispered into Zach's ear. He felt it, the moment Zach started to come.

Zach's body froze, even as his fist kept moving. A shudder ran through him and straight into Kage's cock. Zach's body clamped down on Kage, gripping him even tighter.

Zach came hard, shouting Kage's name. Strands of come slid from the tip of his dick and rolled down over his fingers. Kage murmured encouragement against the shell of his ear.

He was caught off guard when Zach's body went almost completely limp. Kage wrapped his arms around Zach's chest, holding him upright. Reaching behind himself, he snagged one of the hand towels, using it to clean Zach for a second time.

"Easy," Kage soothed, easing Zach to lie on his stomach again. He pressed his forehead to the back of Zach's neck, struggling for self-control.

Taking a deep breath to steady himself, Kage retrieved Zach's discarded pillow and slid it beneath his hips. Again, he twined their fingers, nuzzled Zach's hair, and began to move his hips.

This time, it was Zach who chanted encouraging words as he moved into Kage's thrusts. To Kage's surprise, it was only moments before his balls tightened. Zach's scent, the feel of his skin as he writhed beneath Kage, were simply too much to endure. Kage struggled to hold off, but his body had other ideas, and his hips lost rhythm.

"Oh, fuck, I'm coming," he said, voice raw as his cock pulsed inside Zach's ass. Bolts of electricity rocketed through his system, shooting up his spine. As the first jet of his come flooded the condom tip, Kage shouted in triumph.

Somewhere, Kage lost time. He slowly became aware that he was laying atop Zach's limp body, both of them gasping for breath. Quickly, he pushed himself onto his arms.

"Sorry, I must be heavy," he said. His throat burned and he wondered how much shouting he'd done.

"No, you're fine." Zach's voice was as rough as Kage's.

He eased himself from Zach's body with a hiss. He tossed the condom and collapsed onto the bed. Zach looked at him drowsily from beneath heavy lids. Kage kissed him, draped an arm around his waist, and almost immediately relaxed into sleep.

CHAPTER SIX

Kage awoke with a gasp, sitting straight up in bed. At least he hadn't woken himself up shouting, this time. The dream was always the same: Kage was sitting in the Humvee. A young corporal was his driver. The convoy was ambushed. His Humvee flipped over, trapping him inside. He was forced to stare into the dead eyes of his driver, who had been no more than a boy. His men pulled Kage free of the wreckage as the insurgents closed in around them. Kage dropped to a knee, lifting his weapon to his shoulder. Sighting down the muzzle, he fired at the armed hostile who blindly aimed an AK-47. Kage saw the hostile fall to the pavement, his eyes as dead, and his face just as young as the corporal who had driven his Humvee.

He ran both hands over his face. Already, the dream was fading. Kage should have been the one who died that day. His driver – he couldn't remember his name anymore – was so young, he had so much

promise and hope left in his life. It made no sense that Kage had lived, with such an empty life stretching bleakly in front of him.

Glancing at the clock, Kage saw it was zero three hundred. Something wasn't right. Memories came flooding back, and Kage reached across the bed for Zach. He touched only fabric, but it was still warm.

Searching for sounds in the dark room, Kage thought he heard clothes rustling. It came from outside the bedroom door.

Slipping from the bed, Kage retrieved his briefs and saw Zach's clothing was gone. Stepping into the hallway, he could just make out Zach moving in the dark. It looked like he was getting dressed.

"Hey," he said quietly, voice hoarse from sleep.

Zach startled violently. "Shit!"

"Sorry," Kage said, stepping closer. Disappointment sent a chill through his body. He'd thought Zach was going to stay the night. He *wanted* Zach to stay the night, and maybe that was a mistake.

"You leaving?"

"Yeah, I thought I was supposed to," Zach replied, sounding confused.

"Oh," he replied, running a hand over his short hair in agitation. "I don't remember saying that." Kage struggled to sound neutral.

"You didn't have to." Zach had stopped dressing at least. He stood with his back to the wall.

Kage wished for more light. He wanted to see Zach's face, to try to figure his way through this. "If you want to go, that's cool."

"I didn't think you'd be comfortable sleeping with someone." Zach's tone was matter-of-fact. Despite the darkness, he didn't seem tense or angry.

"I would have said something." Kage tried to match Zach's relaxed tone. "Why wouldn't I be comfortable sleeping with you?"

"You're still tense in crowds and jump at loud noises. I thought you might have nightmares and wouldn't want me to see."

That wasn't the answer Kage had expected. He stood in stunned silence for several moments. The significance of Zach's ability to intuit and understand Kage hit him like a blow to the stomach.

He stepped in, pressing Zach to the wall. Kage clasped Zach's face with both hands and kissed him. Zach gasped in surprise, and Kage inhaled the warm breath. He pushed his chest and hips into Zach, pinning him in place. He put all he was feeling into the kiss: his passion, his affection, and how grateful he was that Zach accepted all of his idiosyncrasies.

"I've already had tonight's nightmare, and I didn't wake up swinging or screaming, so you're safe," he whispered against Zach's mouth, flicking his tongue over his lower lip.

Zach gripped Kage's wrists hard enough to bruise. "I'm sorry that happens to you," he whispered.

Kage didn't want to talk about it anymore. "Are you coming back to bed?"

"If you want me to, yeah." Zach released a breath that sounded like he'd been holding it, waiting for Kage's next move.

Kage took one of Zach's hands, leading him back into the bedroom. Slowly, he undressed Zach again before leading him to the bed. He helped him slide beneath the sheet.

When Kage slid into the bed, Zach lay facing him. Kage drew Zach's top leg up and draped it over his hip. That seemed to unlock something inside of Zach. He slid closer, pressing their chests together, wrapping his arm around Kage's chest. Kage hooked his hand behind Zach's head, cradling it.

He was aware of the moment Zach slid into sleep. Kage didn't follow. His thoughts were swirling. He realized he didn't want to say goodbye to Zach.

Kage was aware that he was difficult to be around sometimes, but he hoped Zach thought he was worth the trouble.

• • •

Kage heard Zach stir. He heard him stumble to the bathroom. He listened to Zach get dressed and all the while, Kage stared at the website on his laptop. He had to trust that the change to his plans would be welcomed.

"There you are," Zach said, leaning on the door sill. "You've been up a while, haven't you?"

He was dressed but still disheveled. Kage found it sexy. He wondered if Zach always looked this cute, the morning after vigorous sex. Kage hoped he'd get to find out.

"Yeah, I had some things to take care of," he answered, closing the laptop. He dried his suddenly moist palms on his jeans.

"Everything okay?" Zach crossed his arms over his chest.

"Yeah, fine," Kage replied hastily. He paused, gathering his nerve. "I canceled the rest of my reservation here and changed my flight home."

"You did?" Zach looked puzzled.

Kage swallowed hard. "There were seats available on the same flight you're on."

"You're flying home with us? Today?" Kage thought he detected hope and pleasure in Zach's expression.

"Yeah." His mouth had gone dry and Kage swallowed again. "I've been here long enough. It's time to go home and be with my family."

Zach smiled. "Did you call your mom?"

Kage grinned. "Yeah, she's pretty happy."

"Is she already planning a homecoming barbecue?" Zach's tone was playful and knowing.

"Before she even hung up the phone." Kage's smile faded and silence stretched between them. "If I invited you to this thing, would you want to come?"

Zach's lips parted in surprise. "Sure." He studied Kage for several moments. "Are you inviting me as a friend?" he asked hesitantly.

"Is that what you want to be?" Kage met Zach's gaze, holding his breath as he waited for the answer.

"No," Zach replied hastily. "No, I want us to be more than friends."
Kage nodded his agreement, unable to form the words.

Zach stepped away from the door, pushing his hands into his front pockets. "We never talked about this, so I didn't ask, are you out to your family?"

"I never said anything, but I think they figured it out," replied Kage.

"What makes you think that?"

Kage nervously rubbed his palms together. "For years, my mom has been mentioning that she's okay with 'alternative lifestyles.'" Kage implied the air quotes. "She's also very careful with pronouns."

Zach took another step closer. "So, you're comfortable confirming their suspicions?"

"I think it's time to tell them directly." Kage didn't want to hide anything about Zach, even if it meant talking about his private life.

Zach lifted his chin slightly, almost like a challenge. "Are you willing to meet my family, too?"

Kage took a deep breath. "Under the right conditions." This was one of those normal, everyday things he had to re-learn how to deal with.

"Yes, of course," Zach agreed readily. "I don't expect you to walk into a family reunion, next week.

My parents prefer casual conversation to the third-degree, anyway."

Kage smiled, nearly euphoric with relief. Of course, Zach understood. "We can figure it out as we go."

Zach pushed the laptop aside, sitting down on the table, in front of Kage. "Are you sure you're ready for all of this?"

Smile fading, dread settled heavily in Kage's belly. "I'm sure. It doesn't sound like you are, though."

Zach pressed both of Kage's hands between his own. "No, that's not..." he gave a frustrated sigh.

"Don't push yourself too fast. I don't need you to be some arbitrary definition of normal."

Kage shook his head. "I don't want everyone constantly worrying about me, or feeling like they're walking on eggshells around me," he said in frustration.

"You can't stop us from worrying," Zach said emphatically. "But I promise I won't censor myself around you. Just don't pretend things are okay, if they're not."

"I feel better now, than when I first got here," Kage insisted. "There are still going to be some bad days, though."

Zach's grip tightened on Kage's hands. "I'm sure there will be. It's okay, though."

Kage's stomach tied itself in knots at Zach's expression. He watched Kage expectantly, eyes shining. He looked smitten. Kage hoped that look would never go away.

"You know, Iraq is an ugly place," Kage said in a rush. "Bad shit happens there." There was more he wanted to say, but Zach stopped him.

"I know," he said firmly. "You wouldn't have nightmares if it was a party over there. Can we just..." Zach released a frustrated breath. "I don't want you to think I don't want to know what happened. Can we just get home, get settled, and enjoy ourselves for a couple more days? Then we can deal with real life."

Kage studied Zach's earnest expression. He believed Zach just wanted some time and wasn't afraid to know the things Kage had done. "Yeah, that's probably a good idea," he admitted. "Since I'll have a lot to deal with right when I get home."

Zach pressed a firm kiss to Kage's lips. "We need to get packed so we can get out of here," he murmured against Kage's mouth. "If we get to the airport early enough, we can probably get our seats moved so we can sit together."

Kage stood, urging Zach to his feet. "Come on! What are you waiting for? Let's get moving."

Zach laughed as he left to get his own packing done.

CHAPTER SEVEN

"I haven't spent a lot of time in the north county," Zach shouted over the crowd. "But yeah, it would be easy to get assigned to Vista Detention for my jail tour. After that, there are always openings at the patrol stations in Vista, San Marcos, or Escondido."

Kage was amazed once again that things just fell into place for Zach and him. "Only if that's what you want. I could move farther south. A commute wouldn't kill me."

"Let me graduate the academy first!" Zach exclaimed with a smile. "That's in Miramar, which is already closer to Oceanside."

Kage knew it was too early to ask Zach to move in with him, but maybe in six months or so, the time would be right.

He followed Zach as he pushed his way through the crowd to the luggage carousel. Matt and Ashley were nearby, also shoving through the press of people. The group shouted to each other, over the typical airport din.

They got lucky when Kage spotted his and Zach's bags, already circling around. Kage had just lifted the handle on his suitcase when he heard someone shout his name.

He turned in confusion, spotting his mother waving like a madwoman from the far edge of the crowd, as she avoided the crush of bodies. He groaned inwardly. Kage thought he'd have more time to prepare for this.

Zach came to stand next to him. "Is that your mom?" he asked, grinning.

"Yeah," replied Kage mournfully. "I told her I was taking a shuttle home but apparently, she couldn't wait that long."

"Should we say goodbye now?" Zach asked.

At first, Kage thought Zach was referring to Matt and the rest of the group. It took him several moments to realize Zach was asking if he should say goodbye to Kage.

"That depends," he said, hoping Zach wasn't trying to make a get-away. "Are you ready to meet my doting mother, several hours earlier than expected?"

"If you're ready, I'm ready," Zach said with a shrug.

Kage realized he might not be ready for this after all. "Well then, let's go meet my mother."

Zach spoke briefly to Matt, who nodded vigorously in reply. When he turned back, Kage held out his hand. Zach took it without hesitation. Wheeling their luggage behind them, Kage and Zach dodged other travelers. They approached Kage's mother, hand-in-hand.

Kage watched his mother's smiling face. She nearly bounced where she stood, her eyes roving over him as if searching for an injury. Her glance darted to Zach, his hand clasped tightly in Kage's, their shoulders brushing. Her expression became curious. Kage saw when she caught sight of their joined hands.

He prepared himself for anger and disapproval. Instead, his mother's smile widened, her eyes shining with pleasure. As Kage led Zach out of the baggage claim area and into the crowd of harried travelers, and reunited friends and family, his mother opened her arms to him.

Kage released his hold on Zach and his suitcase so he could hug his mother. She wrapped her arms around his shoulders and held tight. She greeted him as eagerly as she had when he'd first returned from Iraq. A twinge of guilt twisted Kage's stomach as he realized his mom hadn't just missed him, she'd probably been worried.

"Welcome home," she said, pulling back and pressing a noisy kiss to his cheek. "Again!"

"Thanks, Mom," Kage replied, taking each of her hands in his. "This time, it feels good to be home."

"I'm sorry if we overwhelmed you," she said, looking contrite. "But we're so proud of you and we're so glad you made it home safely."

"I know." Kage pressed a kiss to her forehead. "I just needed to decompress, I think."

"I understand." His mom looked up at him, smirking. "Are you going to introduce me to your friend, now?"

Kage was surprised to feel his face flush. By now he was used to having trouble breathing while his heart raced. Turning, Kage rested his hand in the small of Zach's back, urging him forward.

"Zach, I'd like you to meet my mother; Carol Bennett." Kage rested his other hand on his mom's shoulder. "Mom, this is my friend, Zach..." He was mortified to realize he didn't know Zach's last name. How had that even happened?

"Zach Hailey." Zach took Carol's hand in his own. "It's a pleasure to meet you, Mrs. Bennett."

Kage rubbed a small circle on Zach's spine, in silent thanks for his smooth cover.

"It's wonderful to meet you, too, Zach." Carol clasped Zach's hand with both of hers. "And please call me Carol. Did you and Kage meet in Mexico?"

"Yes, ma'am," Zach replied with a quick glance at Kage.

"I invited Zach to this party you're throwing, later today," Kage told her.

His mom looked at him in confusion. "What party?" Her expression cleared. "For the family to get together and welcome you home? Oh, honey, I wouldn't do that to you." She laughed, cradling his cheek in her palm. "That's tomorrow afternoon. I knew you'd want to get home, unpack, and settle in."

Kage looked at her through narrowed eyes. "When we were on the phone..."

"Sweetie, I was trying to make of the reason I know you fled to Mexico," she said gently. "Your father made me promise to tone it down. So, tomorrow afternoon, and just the immediate family. No friends, no neighbors."

Kage looked at Zach, wondering how the change would affect his plans.

"I admit, that's more convenient," Zach said, smiling. "Travel days always feel stressful and hectic."

"Hey, Zach?" Matt called from the sliding exit doors. "We're going out to catch the shuttle."

"I'd be happy to take you home, Zach," Carol said, surprising Kage.

"I'm out of the way for you, from what Kage says," Zach said hastily.

"I have nothing pressing to do, today," she replied. "And it'll be nice to chat without having to shout over a crowd."

Kage liked the idea of having a little more time with Zach, even if his mother was with them. "Come on," he said to Zach. "Let us take you home."

Zach gave in easily, to Kage's pleasure. They said goodbye to Zach's friends and followed Carol to the parking structure where she'd left her SUV.

Kage loaded both suitcases into the cargo area. As the tailgate clicked shut, his mom held the key out to him.

"What's this?" he asked, taking them hesitantly.

Mom pulled a face. "Kage, you are your father's son. You only think you're hiding the fidgeting, and all the panicked sounds you make are distracting. It's easier to just let you drive." She surprised him further by climbing into the rear seat.

As Zach began to slide into the passenger seat, he said to Carol, "I'm happy to sit in the backseat, ma'am. After all, you're doing me the favor of taking me home."

Kage watched his mother in the rearview mirror as he fastened his seatbelt. The smile she gave Zach looked genuine.

"I'm fine back here. You're a lot taller than I am, and I think Kage would rather have you sit next to him, than his old mother." She gave Kage's shoulder an affectionate squeeze.

"If you're sure, ma'am," Zach said as he fastened his seatbelt.

"My name is Carol, and I'm sure."

Kage started the engine. His mom wasn't just accepting of the fact her son was gay, she was actively encouraging Kage's relationship with a man. He knew it was too much to hope his entire family would behave the same way.

Carol didn't bother with subtlety as she grilled Zach. Her technique rivaled every CIA interrogator Kage had ever seen. Zach held nothing back. He turned in the seat to speak to her directly. It was like Kage wasn't even there.

He focused so intently on the questions his mom asked Zach, hoping she wouldn't embarrass him too much, it took Kage quite a while to realize Zach was on his own recon mission. He was taking advantage of Carol's gregarious manner, and her surprising pride in Kage, to gather intel.

"His sister must have hated him for that," Zach said with a laugh.

"She declared that her life was over," Carole replied. "In typical dramatic, teenage fashion."

"I didn't care if she was pissed at me," Kage interrupted. "That asshole bossed her around and told her she was stupid and worthless. He was an up and coming abuser. Kimberly was better off without him."

"Yes, she realized that," his mom said. "She got over being mad the very next week. But the point of the story isn't that you made your older sister angry. It's that you were only fourteen-years-old and already bigger and stronger than her eighteen-year-old boyfriend. You jumped right in to protect your sister, without a second thought, and you've been doing the same thing, ever since."

Kage grunted in reply, not sure what he was supposed to say.

"Kage has a younger brother, too, doesn't he?" Zach asked Carol.

"Yes. Kerry," she replied.

"Oh, no," Zach sounded disappointed. "You're one of *those* moms, aren't you? Kim, Kage, and Kerry?"

"Guilty!" Carol declared as both of them broke into laughter.

Kage bit back a smile.

"Kage was a typical big brother to Kerry," his mom said. "But they're so different from each other, they were never close."

"Kerry got the brains," said Kage. "I'm all brawn."

Carol chastised him at the same time Zach landed a light punch on Kage's arm. He laughed his words off as a joke, surprised at the vehemence of their response.

"I have one older brother," Zach said. "We've always been friends so we're mutually protective. We're also mutually antagonistic." His tone turned dry.

"No one can push your buttons quite like a sibling," Carol mused.

Kage exited the freeway at Alvarado. Zach faced forward to provide driving directions. He directed Kage to a modest apartment complex, like so many other complexes in So Cal. Multiple two-story buildings, painted in various shades of tan and brown, formed a large square. Kage knew if he entered through the pedestrian gate, the buildings would overlook a mundane courtyard with a kidney-shaped pool. Metal and concrete stairs led to the second floor of each building. It was pretty typical for a college student.

Zach directed Kage to a parking spot designated for visitors.

"Zach, honey, it was wonderful to meet you," Carol said effusively. "I'm so glad you'll be joining us tomorrow, so Kage's brother and sister can meet you."

Kage climbed out of the SUV and didn't hear Zach's reply. Opening the tailgate, he retrieved Zach's suitcase. He surprised himself at how reluctant he was to drop Zach off and leave.

He shut the tailgate, lifting the handle on Zach's suitcase, ready to wheel it behind.

"I've got it from here," Zach said, coming around the rear of the SUV. He covered Kage's hand on the luggage handle with his own. "You don't have to walk me to my door, this time. But I really appreciate you bringing me home."

"I want to walk you to your door, for the same reason I always want to walk you to your door," Kage replied quietly. They'd exchanged cell numbers on the plane, so he was out of legitimate reasons to linger.

Zach stepped in closer, until Kage felt the heat of his body. "I don't want your mom sitting alone and bored, in the car. Otherwise, I'd drag you into my apartment and lock the door behind us."

Kage smiled, his chest tightening pleasantly. He ran the backs of his fingers down Zach's cheek. "I'll call you when I get home."

"Good," Zach whispered. He tilted his face toward Kage, like he was waiting for a kiss.

The urge to kiss Zach as powerful. Kage was too aware of his mother sitting right inside the car next to them. He glanced quickly through the rear window. He was just able to see his mom through the dark tint of the glass. She sat facing forward, talking animatedly on her cell phone. Turning back, Kage cupped Zach's cheek in one palm, bringing their mouths together. Zach met him eagerly, lips parting under Kage's. Their tongues met eagerly, rubbing against each other briefly, before they both pulled back self-consciously.

It was enough for now.

"Call me," Zach whispered. He pressed another quick kiss to Kage's lips before turning to head toward his apartment.

As Kage climbed back into the driver's seat, his mom quickly ran around to the passenger seat and slid in. He smiled at her, recognizing her attempt to give Kage and Zach a little privacy to say good-bye.

"You must have enjoyed yourself," Carol said as Kage pulled out into traffic. "You looked relaxed and tan."

"Do I?" he asked, surprised she wasn't grilling him about Zach.

"Did you just happen to meet Zach on your trip? Or did you go there to meet up with him?"

Kage snorted a laugh. "We just met."

"I like him. He's very friendly and charming."

He waited for her to say more, but his mom stayed silent.

"What will Kim and Kerry say?" Kage asked, not looking at his mom.

From the corner of his eye, he saw her look at him sharply. "I can't speak for them, but there's no reason they both won't like him." She paused. "But that's not what you're asking, is it?"

Kage blew out a harsh breath, not sure how to answer. He still couldn't look at his mother. He was afraid of her answer, whatever it was. He had no clue what his response to her should be, no matter what she said.

"If you hadn't avoided talking about it for so long, Kage, it wouldn't be an eight-hundred-pound gorilla, now," his mom said, a hint of anger in her voice. "You're *gay*, Kage, let's finally put it out there in the open. I don't pretend to know what it's like for you, and I'm sure it's been difficult at times. But I know I've made it clear that the subject would not be met with hostility, when you brought it up. Whatever knots you tied yourself up in, you did so needlessly."

Kage gnawed at the inside of his cheek. He felt like a kid again, being reprimanded for doing something he knew better than to do. "Just because you're okay with it, Mom, doesn't mean the rest of the family is. It seemed easier to pretend, than to force everybody to deal with it."

"I had a pretty good idea when you were still in middle-school," she said dryly. "We've had time to adjust."

Kage looked at his mom in surprise. "How?" he asked incredulously.

Carol waved a hand dismissively. "I just had a feeling so I started watching and listening closely," she replied. "I can't tell you exactly. I just knew."

"I wish you'd said something." Kage couldn't help sounding a little annoyed.

"I didn't want you to feel backed into a corner!" Carol declared heatedly. "I thought you were going to say something when they repealed that ridiculous Don't Ask Don't Tell. I half expected you to do exactly what you did today, show up with a man in tow like it was nothing."

Kage silently considered her words. He'd been worried about how Zach felt, how he would react, what he wanted from Kage. How his family would react to his relationship with Zach had been far down on the list of things that had him stressed.

"Maybe," Kage said, pausing to clear his throat and run his tongue over his dry lips. "Maybe, on some level, I've been waiting until I had someone I wanted to bring home."

His mom said nothing at first but stared out the windscreen for several moments. Finally, she nodded. "That does sound very much like you. And I'm grateful you aren't someone who shows up with a different person every time we see you."

Kage tightened his grip on the steering wheel. He was pretty sure his brother and sister hadn't had to deal with this same thing.

"And I feel the same way about your siblings, too," Carol said, before Kage thought of something to say that wasn't hostile. "It has nothing to do with you being gay. In fact, before Kerry met Grace, he did quite a bit of casual dating. This was before you were stationed at Pendleton, so you don't know what he was like. I finally told him I was too old to be learning a new name and face with that kind of frequency." His mom chuckled. "Kimberly told him that if he couldn't have dinner with his family without having to bring a date, he should look into therapy."

Kage laughed. "That sounds like Kim."

They sat in comfortable silence for several minutes. When Kage exited the freeway near his own house, he knew he was running out of time.

"You've told me how you feel about...about me...about the fact I'm gay." Despite the number of times he'd said it, this time, the word felt strange on Kage's tongue. "If someone's going to give us shit, I just want to warn Zach." He waited for his mom to chastise him for swearing.

"The topic came up between your father and me, when you were still in high school." His mom surprised him when she didn't comment on his language. "It took him several years to actually accept it, but he did, eventually. Kim and Kerry each figured it out on their own. They've asked me for confirmation, which I haven't been able to do. But the only reason either of them brought it up, was they didn't want to make an incorrect assumption, either way."

Kage sighed heavily, making the turn onto his own street. He'd always felt comfortable around his family. Some part of him had to have picked up on their unspoken acceptance.

His driveway was narrow, leading past his house to the single car garage at the rear of the property. It was small and modest, but it was a house Kage could afford to own on a gunny's salary. His Jeep was in the garage, so he pulled all the way up beside the house.

Kage shut off the engine and unfastened his seatbelt, but he made no move to exit the vehicle. His mother sat quietly beside him.

"I'm still dealing with this last deployment," he confessed quietly. "Some shit went down and I'm even more twisted up than I was after the previous ones."

"Just promise me one thing." Carol turned to look directly at Kage. Her tone said this was a demand, not a request. "If you ever feel the urge to hurt yourself, or someone else, you will call me before you do anything."

Kage wanted to scoff at how serious she was making this sound. He stopped himself. The news was full of veterans losing it on other people. Some of the Marines Kage had served with previously had eaten the barrels of their own guns. His mom was right to worry.

"I promise," he said, completing the connection his mom was trying to establish.

She gave him a watery smile.

Kage climbed out of the SUV, leaving the door open. He retrieved his suitcase and closed the tailgate. He mom stood watching, still smiling at him. If there was something Kage should say to her, he didn't know what it was. She saved him by simply opening her arms. Kage pulled her narrow frame into a hug, holding her tight against him. She buried her face in his chest and rocked, as if he was still a child who could fit on her lap.

His mom pulled back abruptly, grasped his face in both her hands, and pressed a loud kiss to his cheek. "I love you, Kage," she said fiercely. "No matter what."

He swallowed against his suddenly tight throat as his mom stepped past him and climbed into her car. Kage wheeled his suitcase to his front door as his mom backed into the street. She waved one last time before disappearing down the street.

CHAPTER EIGHT

Kage opened the door to his parents' house, stepping aside for Zach to enter. Carol had insisted they not bring anything, but Zach had ignored her. He carried a pretty decent bottle of wine and a case of damn good beer. Kage led the way into the kitchen. As they put the beer in the refrigerator, happy party sounds drifted in through the sliding screen door. His nieces and nephews screamed and squealed, despite Kim's cautions to behave.

Closing the fridge door, Kage took a deep breath. "Ready?" He rolled his shoulders, trying to ease the tension.

"Yeah," Zach answered with a hesitant smile. "Your mom told you they're all okay with this, right? It'll be okay, Kage. Try to relax."

He couldn't see Zach's eyes behind his sunglasses. Kage had no idea why Zach thought he was nervous about this. One of the kids let loose a blood-curdling scream. Kage jumped, taking a step back from Zach. His heart slammed against his ribs, his skin prickling with the rush of adrenaline.

Fuck.

"Okay, this isn't about your family," Zach said quietly. "Would it help to hold my hand? Or do you need space?"

Kage ran his hands over his short hair. He'd taken his clippers to it last night when he no longer recognized his own reflection. Children in Iraq didn't scream out of joy.

"Hand," he said brusquely, holding his own out for Zach to take. "I'll tell you if I need space. I hope being outside will help."

Without a word, Zach grasped Kage's outstretched hand and held on.

Heading for the sliding screen, Kage pulled Zach along behind him. They stepped out into the bright, warm sunshine. A strong breeze kept the heat from being oppressive to Kage's relief.

"Uncle Kage!" Kerry's daughter, Jodie, splashed her way up the steps of the pool. She ignored everyone's shouts not to run, her small feet slapping wetly on the pool deck. She held her arms out as she ran, brilliantly colored water wings staying snuggly in place.

Jesus, she'd grown. It always amazed him how much kids changed in six months, let alone a year. Despite how much she'd grown since Kage had last seen her, she was still so tiny.

He caught her on the run, grasping her beneath her arms and sweeping her up. He clasped her to his chest as her little arms wrapped tight around his neck, her water wings pressing against his face. Water from her wet swimsuit soaked through his muscle shirt, but Kage didn't care, he'd dry quickly in this heat.

"Welcome home, Uncle Kage." Jodie's words were muffled by her water wing and Kage's neck.

"Thank you, Jodie," Kage whispered, pressing a kiss to her little, blonde head.

He shifted his niece to his hip to make way for Kim's embrace. Kage wrapped his free arm around her waist as Kim's arms went around his neck.

With her head on his shoulder, Kim said, "I missed you. I'm so glad you made it back okay."

Kage pressed a quick kiss to her temple as she pulled back to let Kerry step up.

"Come on, Jodie," Kerry said, taking his reluctant daughter from Kage and settling her on his own hip. "You need to give everyone a chance to greet Uncle Kage."

Even as he took Kerry's outstretched hand, Kage was aware Zach standing just behind him. He wanted his brother and sister to meet Zach, but before he could say a word, Kerry tugged his hand to pull him closer. Kage was stunned when his brother kissed his cheek and squeezed his hand tight.

"God, it's good to have you back," Kerry said, giving Kage's arm an affectionate slap. He stepped aside to clear the way for the next person, still smiling warmly.

Kerry's wife, Grace, hugged him next. Kage was relieved to hear his mom greet Zach enthusiastically. He heard his mom introduce Zach to Kim and Kerry, so he didn't hear what Grace was saying to him. Kage murmured something polite to her as she stepped out of his arms.

"Welcome back, Kage," said Ray, Kim's husband. He shook Kage's hand and gave him a wry smile. "You look like Mexico did you some good."

Kage returned Ray's smile and relaxed a little. "Thanks, man. I think I'm glad to be back, now." He got the idea Ray understood a little about feeling smothered by the ones who love you.

Finally, Kage turned toward Zach. A goofy grin spread across Kage's face at the sight of Zach laughing and talking animatedly with his family. Ray joined the group and Kim introduced him to Zach. Kage tensed when Kim easily referred to Zach as his boyfriend. Ray showed no surprise, to Kage's relief, as he gave Zach a friendly handshake.

Kage tried to gauge how Zach felt about Kim calling him a boyfriend. Zach turned to smile at Kage as he listened to whatever Kerry was saying. The last of Kage's tension drained away. He stepped in next to Zach, put a hand in the small of his back, and leaned into his side, slightly. Standing among his family while he touched Zach felt like the right thing to do.

Everyone laughed when Zach finished a story about Matt's antics during one of their excursions in Mexico. Jodie unexpectedly broke into the laughter.

"Do I call you Uncle Zach, now?" she blurted with an innocent but curious expression.

Denial was on the tip of Kage's tongue, but Zach answered first. "Only if you want to, but you don't have to."

"Uncle Ray gets called Uncle Ray, so you get called Uncle Zach," Jodie replied with complete aplomb. Kage's family laughed at the little girl's firm pronouncement.

"I think that answers that," Carol declared, bestowing the entire group with a wide smile.

"Hey, Kage!" his father called from his official place in front of the barbeque grill. "Why don't you bring your father a beer?"

"Oh, lord, I've completely lost my manners!" his mom said with embarrassment. "I forgot to offer Zach something to drink."

"I'm fine, please don't worry about it," Zach told her.

Kage laughed at his mother's chagrin. "I'll take care of it," he said, twining his fingers with Zach's. "Since I've been summoned by Dad." Kage led Zach to a nearby cooler where he snagged three cold beer bottles from the ice. Handing one to Zach he said, "My dad doesn't really need me to bring him a beer. He just wants to talk and he can't leave the grill."

Kage's older nieces and nephews shouted greetings from where they splashed around in the pool. He'd have to jump in and spend some time playing with the kids, after he talked to his dad. Kim's two sons, and Kerry's one, liked to team up against Jodie and Kim's daughter. Kage sometimes helped the girls even the odds.

He handed his dad one of the bottles, confused when his father immediately set it down on the grill's small table. He braced himself to introduce Zach, but Kage was caught completely off guard when his dad pulled him in for a fierce hug. Kage's throat tightened at the overt display of affection. His father was free with affectionate squeezes to the shoulder and slaps to the back, also subjecting the kids to tousled hair. Kage could count on one hand, the number of times his dad had been so blatant with his love and approval.

"It's good to have you home, Kage," his father said, voice rough with emotion. "I'm proud of you, son."

Kage could only nod in reply. When his father delivered strong slaps to his back, Kage knew they were both affected by the gesture. Finally, his dad released him, quickly turning away to retrieve his beer, keeping his face hidden.

Clearing his throat, Kage opened his own beer. He blinked rapidly as he tilted his back to take a long drink. The heat of Zach's body was suddenly against his side.

Kage cleared his throat again. "Dad, I want you to meet my friend, Zach Hailey. Zach, my father, Todd Bennett."

"It's an honor to meet you, sir," Zach said quietly, shaking Todd's offered hand.

"The honor's mine, Zach," his dad said. "Glad you could join us, today."

It was that easy. All of Kage's concerns about his family accepting him, and accepting Zach, faded like they'd never existed at all.

* * *

Kage pulled into his garage and shut off the Jeep.

"I like your family," Zach said as he opened the passenger door and climbed out.

Kage followed. "They sure as hell like you." Stepping out of the garage, Kage opened the small panel next to the door and keyed in the code that activated the rolling door. As the garage closed, he led Zach to the back door of his house.

"They're so proud of you, they've run out of ways to show it," Zach said with a chuckle as they entered the house.

Kage thought that was overstating things, but he let it slide. He had other things in mind. He led Zach through the dark house, to his bedroom. Zach's overnight bag lay on the floor at the foot of the bed, where they'd left it earlier. Kage turned on the lights and lowered the dimmer switch, casting the room in a soft, dim light.

Tugging Zach close with a fist in his tank top, Kage placed a gentle kiss on his mouth. Despite his family's acceptance, he hadn't quite been able to do this in front of them. Maybe he'd get there, eventually.

Zach leaned into Kage, his arms sliding around to Kage's back. Kage swallowed his soft sigh of pleasure, licking into Zach's mouth and teasing his tongue. He skimmed his palms down Zach's back until he could grip his firm ass. Kage massaged gently, pressing their hips together so their bodies touched at all points.

Kage lifted his arms when Zach tugged at his shirt, letting the fabric be pulled up and off. He hovered over Zach, their mouths nearly touching, licking playfully at his lips, and tangling their tongues. Zach complied easily when Kage pulled his tank top over his head. As soon as Kage stripped him of the garment, Zach stepped in and pressed their naked chests together.

Zach made a quiet sound that resembled a purr. The way he rubbed himself against the front of Kage's body was like a cat. Kage cradled Zach's face, holding him steady for a deep, lingering kiss. He gripped Zach's chin firmly with one hand, tilting his head back roughly and baring his throat. Kage licked the side of Zach's neck, nipping sharply at the sensitive skin. Zach groaned, breath coming in gasps, his fingers digging into Kage's sides.

Sliding his free hand down Zach's firm chest and along the sharp cuts of his stomach, Kage reached for the waist of his shorts. Kage bit lightly at the place where Zach's neck and shoulder joined.

"Oh fuck," Zach whispered harshly, his body jolting against Kage's. Quickly, Kage freed the button of Zach's shorts. He lowered the zipper and slipped his fingers beneath the low waistband of Zach's briefs. Kissing gently at the corners of Zach's mouth, Kage slid his palm down the length of Zach's hardening cock.

With a shuddering exhale, Zach reached between their bodies. Kage pushed his hands away when Zach tried to open Kage's fly. Zach made a sound of protest that sent a rush of blood flooding into Kage's growing erection.

He kept his grip on Zach's chin, tilting is face higher. Zach's moan was needy, and he shivered again.

"Do you like this?" Kage asked, just above a whisper. He watched Zach's changing expressions as Kage started stroking him again.

"Yes." Zach's response was slow, like it was a struggle to focus on Kage's words. He watched Kage through heavy lidded eyes, his pupils blown wide with desire.

Kage adjusted his angle, wrapping his hand around Zach's cock. He stroked gently, several times, watching Zach's features shift with the different sensations. He nipped at Zach's lower lip, feeling each of his harsh exhalations. The flush on Zach's face darkened, his fingers on Kage's ribs gripping harder.

Using his wrist to push the waist of Zach's briefs out of the way, Kage drew Zach's hard-on into the open air. Slowly, Kage jacked him, keeping his grip light. Zach's mouth fell open and his brows drew together in a frown. Kage plunged his tongue past Zach's lips, teasing and urging Zach to lick back at him.

Zach moved his hips rhythmically against Kage's fist. Kage smiled against Zach's mouth, swallowing his frustrated grunts and sighs. Kage enjoyed the silky feel of Zach's cock in his palm. He teased the slick, sensitive skin with his fingertips. Zach thrust against him, circling his hips, urging Kage to speed his hand. He denied Zach the added friction he silently begged for.

Kage had Zach where he wanted him. He kept him skating the edge of pleasure, leaving him needy and wanting. Kage placed open-mouthed kisses down the length of Zach's throat. The desperate, wanton sounds Zach made had Kage's erection pushing hard against the front of his shorts. He ached to push himself deep into Zach's body. He knew that when he finally did, Zach would be open and ready for him.

Releasing Zach's chin, Kage buried his fingers in the soft hair at the back of his head. He pressed his lips to Zach's ear and whispered, "God, I want to fuck you so bad."

A violent shudder ran the length of Zach's body, and he choked on his own breath. Grasping at the back of Kage's neck with one hand, Zach tried to tug him closer. Kage resisted, knowing it would ratchet up Zach's tension and arousal. He released Zach's cock, using both hands to push Zach's shorts down over his hips. When Zach reached for Kage's fly again, Kage grasped his wrists tightly. Taking a step back, he pulled Zach with him. Awkwardly, Zach stepped out of his sandals and kicked out of his shorts.

Walking backward, Kage tugged Zach along with him. He stopped at the side of his bed, pushing Zach down onto it. Kage watched Zach slide into the center of the bed, quickly kicking out of his own sandals, shoving his shorts down, and out of the way.

Zach's expression was hungry. Kage stood naked, his cock standing out rigidly from between his thighs, letting Zach look at him. He gave his erection a couple of lazy strokes, smiling at Zach to add to the teasing. Zach's throat worked as he swallowed hard several times. He moved sluggishly, like his limbs were heavy, as he slowly started to turn onto his stomach. Moving quickly, Kage knelt on the bed beside Zach, stopping him with a hand pressed firmly to his stomach.

"Uh uh." Kage smiled wickedly. He grabbed Zach's upraised knees, pushing them apart, and sliding between his thighs. "I want you just like this." Kage braced himself over Zach's body.

Zach ran his hands along Kage's ribs, and up over his back. He lifted a leg, skimming Kage's thigh and hip with his calf. Kage resisted Zach's grip on his ass, urging him to lower his hips. He grinned down at Zach, pleased to see his growing frustration written clearly on his face.

Kage pressed his own hard-on against Zach's, grinding against him. He saw Zach's flush deepen, watched his eyelids grow heavy. Kage circled his hips, dragging his cock along the length of Zach's.

When Zach's soft lips parted, his mouth falling open enticingly, Kage knew he was verging on desperate.

"Please," Zach pleaded, thrusting upward into Kage.

"Please what?" Kage demanded. He stopped moving against Zach, teasing him mercilessly.

"Please...fuck me." Zach's voice was choked.

Kage pumped his hips once. "You want me inside you?" He liked having Zach desperate and needy. It touched something inside of Kage that had been long buried under a core of aggression.

Zach strained against Kage, chasing the delicious friction with his hips. "Yeah." He settled back down, his body still vibrating with tension.

"You wanna feel me deep inside your ass?" Kage thrust himself hard against Zach's body several times. He smiled at Zach's eager response to the silent promise.

"Yeah." Zach's reply was pleading. His willing compliance added fuel to Kage's arousal, taking him to the brink of his self-control.

Kage propped himself on one hand, reaching his other between their bodies. He slid his fingers back behind Zach's heavy sac, trailing a fingertip along his taint. Zach lifted his hips compulsively, bringing his clenched hole up to meet Kage's finger.

He watched Zach battle his own desire, struggling to lie still beneath Kage. "Is this where you want me?" Kage circled his finger lightly against Zach's opening. "You want me to shove my cock into your tight hole?"

"Yes. Fuck, please!" Zach nearly sobbed, arching his neck and throwing his head back. A shudder raced through him, vibrating into Kage.

Opening the bedside table, Kage retrieved the things he needed. He set the items between his own legs. Gripping Zach behind his knees, Kage pushed them upward. "Hold yourself open for me," he said firmly.

Obediently, Zach grasped his own knees, pulling himself open for Kage. His hard cock lay against his belly, ball sac hanging low, hovering just above his asshole. Kage enjoyed the tantalizing view, his dick pulsed, pre-come leaking from the tip. His need to give Zach the pleasure he begged for was drowning out Kage's own desire.

Retrieving the lube, Kage let a thick drop land on Zach's clenching fissure. He chuckled when Zach hissed and jumped slightly. Kage liked the way Zach's hole tightened briefly, loosening again as he relaxed. With his thumb, Kage pushed experimentally at Zach's opening. He slid easily into Zach's body, his ass opening right up and taking Kage in. Zach moaned quietly in pleasure.

"That's so good," he murmured to Zach. "I like you all relaxed and ready for my cock."

Zach's erection jumped against his belly, leaving a shiny wet smear on his skin. Kage coated his middle finger in lube. Slowly, he pushed his finger into Zach's ass. There was no resistance, Zach's body taking Kage's finger inside easily. He pushed in deep, pressing the last knuckle hard against Zach's opening.

With a filthy groan, Zach gave in, relaxing completely. His legs fell to his sides, opening him up even wider. Kage pulled out of Zach's ass, and slicked two fingers. He slid them smoothly into Zach's hole. Pulling them out to the tips, Kage tugged slightly, stretching Zach's rim.

With his hands fisted in the sheet beneath him, Zach moaned in time with the rhythm of Kage's hand. Adding lube to three fingers, Kage thoroughly slicked Zach's body, working him loose and open. Kage tapped Zach's gland a few times, with the tip of his finger. Zach gasped, arching his spine off the bed. His cock darkened in color, twitching violently against his belly.

Kage took a deep, shaky breath. He loved the look of ecstasy on Zach's face, his brows drawn together in a frown that showed his pleasure. Kage loved the way he could make Zach shudder. He reveled in his power and control of Zach's body. With the glide of his fingertip over the sweet spot deep in Zach's ass, Kage made Zach gasp for breath, his chest heaving with each inhalation.

"I'm gonna fuck you now." Kage's voice was rough. He wondered if Zach could sense the tremor.

"Please," Zach said in a hoarse whisper, watching Kage from beneath heavy lids. He wet his lips hastily, his pink tongue sliding over his reddened lips. He reached a hand toward Kage, letting it fall back to the bed as if he thought better of the move.

"I want to feel your hands on me," Kage said in his raspy voice.

Zach lifted both hands, running his palms up Kage's arms, and down his chest. "Would you fuck me? Please?" he pleaded quietly. "I wanna feel you inside me, please."

Kage pushed into Zach's strong hands, enjoying the rough scrape of calluses along his skin. "Yeah? Are you ready for me? You might need more prep." His taunt got him the desired response when Zach's fingers dug into his ribs. Kage slid his fingers from Zach's ass, reaching for the condom packet.

"No!" Zach cried out, his eyes going wide. "I'm ready. Please."

Kage's grin faltered, and he fumbled the condom. Zach gripped Kage's hips, trying to tug him forward. That was a better response than he'd expected. Zach writhed against him again, forcing Kage to struggle with the rubber before he finally managed to roll it down his shaft.

"Spread yourself open for me," Kage demanded. He propped both hands on either side of Zach's head. "She me how much you want me. How much you want me to fuck you."

Before Kage even finished issuing his orders, Zach drew his knees up toward his chest. When he dropped his legs toward his sides, he opened himself wide. Kage pushed his hips forward, Zach's skin hot against the fronts of his thighs. Zach canted his hips, lifting his ass to encourage Kage.

With slow, steady thrusts, Kage slid his cock through the cleft of Zach's ass. The head of Kage's erection grazed Zach's hole. Quiet, frustrated sounds escaped Zach, as he struggled to get Kage inside of him.

"Guide me in," Kage said breathlessly, nudging Zach's opening with his cockhead.

Immediately, Zach gripped Kage's dick with trembling fingers. His used his other hand to grip Kage's hip. With a firm, steady push of his hips, Kage breached Zach's body. His cock slipped past Zach's ring of clenched muscles.

"Oh, fuck," Zach said with a harsh exhale. He lifted his shoulders up off the bed, gripping Kage's hips with both hands. Falling back against the pillow, Zach clenched around Kage's erection. "Yeah, like that."

Kage flexed his hips, working himself deep into Zach's body. He pulled out to the tip, then fucked into Zach, burying his cock to the hilt. Zach clung to Kage, moving against him eagerly, his frown deepening in concentration. Kage slid so easily into Zach's ass, settling so deep and tight, it was a perfect fit.

Zach's expression was blissful, making the ache in Kage's chest tighten. Lowering himself to cover Zach's body with his own, Kage nuzzled at Zach's earlobe and the moist skin of his neck. Zach arched up into him. He gave himself over to Kage's control so easily, his trust unquestioning. Kage was as amazed as he was honored, to be the one Zach gave himself over to, like this.

He submitted to Kage's dominance over his body, but Zach wasn't passive. Kage took his own pleasure from the ecstasy he brought Zach. He loved the feel of Zach's warmth against him, the primal sounds he made. The more Kage restrained him, the more he pushed Zach's body around, the more eager and enthusiastic he became.

Kage gripped Zach's biceps and pressing them to the bed. He pressed their palms together, twining their fingers. Kage stretched Zach's arms over his head, firmly pinning him in place. Zach's grip on

Kage's fingers was so tight, it almost hurt. Kage thrust his hips harder, shoving his cock deeper into Zach's ass. The sound of their meeting skin grew louder, melding with Zach's strident cries of pleasure.

The moment Zach was restrained, he came even more alive. Kage felt powerful, not because of Zach's submission, and not because Kage was in control. Zach knew it would be easy for Kage to harm him, but he trusted Kage to only bring him pleasure. It was heady, humbling, and a huge fucking turn on.

Kage nipped at Zach's hammering pulse point, soothing the sting with swipes of his tongue. Kage's body vibrated with the strength of the tremors rolling through Zach's frame. The skin along Zach's jaw and chin rasped against Kage's tongue. The growth of his beard was slight, but just rough enough that Kage's lips tingled.

"You're gonna come for me, Zach," Kage growled, surprising himself. "Come for me, right now, with my cock in your ass." His order was supposed to drive Zach crazy, but it also set off a sparkling light show against the backs of own eyelids.

"Oh...fuck...I'm trying...I want to." Zach's harsh whispers held a high pitch of desperation.

Kage lifted his head to watch Zach's mobile features race through myriad expressions. He delighted in his own taunt, watching in fascination as Zach struggled to please him.

"I'm waiting, Zach." Kage's words were broken by the force of his thrusts into Zach's body. "I told you to come. Now. Thought you wanted to make me happy."

"Trying…I'm trying…getting closer…getting close." Zach drew his brows together as frustration destroyed his concentration.

"You're making me wait." Kage feigned his anger and disappointment. He slowed his hips, barely sliding in and out of Zach's hole. It was killing him to go this slow, but he was amazed at how it raised Zach's arousal even higher. "You must want to disappoint me."

"No!" Zach sounded like he'd taken a physical blow. "If I touch myself. Need to touch my dick. Please. Wanna do this for you."

Christ, Zach was so fucking sexy when he begged like that. "So do it," Kage hissed into Zach's ear. "Stroke your cock, if that'll make you come. Will touching your own dick make you come, now?" He flicked his tongue over the shell of Zach's ear.

The grip of Zach's right hand loosened hesitantly. Kage released him. Zach reached awkwardly between their two bodies, immediately working himself in a fast rhythm. His eyes widened, his jaw fell slack, and he met Kage's eyes with an intense gaze. Zach's body tightened, his inner muscles firmly gripping Kage's erection.

"Are you close now?" Whispering his question, Kage wove his fingers into Zach's hair, fisting the silky strands. Using his grip to hold Zach's face still, Kage kept his lips just out of Zach's reach. "I expect you to be close. I want you to come for me, right now." He breathed in each of Zach's heated exhales. Kage buried himself all the way in Zach's ass, pulling back teasingly slow.

"Faster...please...harder." Zach kept up stroking his cock at a fast pace. The rough sound of skin sliding against skin tightened Kage's belly. "Please...move faster..."

"You wanna get fucked?" Kage demanded. "You'd like me to fuck you hard? You gonna come now? If I pound your ass, fast and hard?"

"Yes! Oh god, yes," Zach cried breathlessly, in between deep, shuddering breaths. "I want...so close...for you..."

Kage rose up and thrust forward forcefully, sinking roughly into Zach's body. The slick heat of Zach's ass enveloped Kage's cock. They were both slick with sweat, so the skin of Kage's thighs met Zach's ass cheeks with a loud slap. Beneath him, Zach arched off the bed, then stilled, not even breathing. His frame was filled with tension, as his climax finally started to roll over him.

Just as Zach came apart in his arms, he locked eyes with Kage. It was a single, perfect moment for Kage, as he started to tumble over the cliff after Zach. Warm fluid splashed onto his belly. His cock was held tight by Zach's clenched inner muscles. Kage made a sound that more animal than human, surprising himself, as his balls tucked themselves tight against his body.

"Oh fuck, I'm coming," Zach cried desperately, his hand still furiously working his dick. "Like you wanted. Do you feel me? Coming for you. Just for you."

With a final thrust, Kage slammed into Zach's ass, his own orgasm rocketing through him. "You got your spunk all over me," he managed to gasp. "Fucking made me come, too." Kage couldn't help but gloat, as he watched Zach shudder helplessly through his climax. "Love the way your ass grabs onto my cock, like it doesn't wanna let me go."

Still breathing hard, Zach began to relax. His hand stilled on his cock. He gave Kage a crooked smile, watching him from beneath heavy lids. "How the fuck did you figure out how to push all my buttons at once?"

Kage released Zach, settling down beside him as they both stretched their well-used bodies. He chuckled, despite the sticky, sweaty mess they were spreading. "How the fuck is it possible that doing what pushes my buttons, pushes yours, too?"

"Better pace ourselves, we might break each other." Zach was still grinning his lopsided grin. His expression was soft as his eyes roamed over Kage's face.

"I'll be sure to repair any accidental damage I might do to you," Kage whispered. He placed a soft kiss at the corner of Zach's mouth, moving along the edge of his jaw.

Zach sighed deeply, sounding completely content. His eyes slid shut, but his lips still curved upward in a small smile. "That's a fair arrangement," he whispered.

Kage carefully slid out of Zach's arms, climbing slowly from the bed. He disposed of the condom and wet a cloth with warm water. Zach moved compliantly as Kage gently cleaned him of sweat, slick, and come. He expected to feel awkward. Kage almost never had opportunities to be...soft; to show any tenderness. Zach made it easy for Kage to look after him, though.

When he'd freshened them both, Kage hung up the cloth and shut off all the lights. He tucked Zach under the sheet, sliding in beside him. Opening his arms, Kage folded Zach into his embrace, waiting for him to settle down enough to sleep. He heard Zach's deep sigh, just before his entire body went lax. Everything about Zach said he was satisfied and contented. There was no need for words between them.

Realization settled over Kage, leaving him warm and at peace. He should be scared shitless. Instead, he placed a soft kiss in Zach's fragrant hair. Kage found it so easy to show Zach tenderness because it was returned effortlessly. There was no clinging, no demands for promises. For the very first time, Kage's every need was met, because what he needed, was just what Zach needed to give.

CHAPTER NINE

It's a convoy, like all the others Kage been assigned to in Iraq. They're way outside the wire. The road is straight and flat. Kage is riding in the passenger seat of the third Humvee. The day is sunny and bright, visibility is good in all directions.

There are structures on either side of the road, approximately 275 meters out. They're traveling at around 80 kph. Kage is aware of the individuals walking along the side of the road, but none are suspicious. Most are old men, women, and children. The young men always hide. It comes out of nowhere. Kage's only warning of the ambush is the sight of several RPG trails. He knows it's coming, but still he's stunned, violently jarred by the impact of an RPG on his poorly armored Humvee. For several endless, agonizing moments, Kage is blind. His ears ring from the concussion of the blast. The vehicle rolls several times, thankfully coming to rest upright, on its tires. The Hillbilly armor is possibly the only thing saving Kage from being crushed. The screams of wounded and dying Marines surround him, punching through the blast-induced ringing. He reaches for his weapon, but his arm hurts, his fingers numb. Kage tries to open the door of the Humvee, but it refuses to budge. He blinks several times, struggling to see out the cracked, dirt-caked windshield. Instead, it only blurs his vision around the edges.

Kage turns his head to ask Morrison, his driver, if they can egress through the driver's door. Morrison no longer has his entire face. Kage realizes the side of his own face is warm and wet, covered in the splattered flesh and brain matter of his Humvee driver. He can't look away from Morrison's staring, sightless eyes.

Sounds of battle rage around him. Marines shout at one another. Something nearby is on fire, the heat is intense, and growing hotter. It's a familiar and deadly chaos that Kage knows he should be a part of. His entire body aches, and his head hurts so much, he's ready to puke. The smell of charred human flesh raises bile in the back of his throat.

The door of Kage's Humvee jerks open with a tortured squeak. Marines are there, tugging him out of the wreckage. Insurgents press their attack. Kage sees movement on the road ahead, and he reacts as he's been trained. He drops down onto one knee, selecting targets and firing in controlled bursts. Even as he kills a hostile who is aiming an AK-47 right at him, a part of Kage's brain recognizes it's just a kid. He's surrounded by wounded civilians, all screaming in pain as they reach toward him for help he can't provide. Beside him is a dead body. Kage doesn't want to look at its face, because he knows what he'll see. He has to, though. Kage looks down into the wide, vacant, staring eyes of a young boy, the entire side of his skull is blown away.

Screams.

There were screams all around Kage. They were so close and so loud; it was like they were in his head. He struggled to reach his weapon, but he couldn't find it. His throat was raw, burning when he swallowed. He searched blindly, feeling all around himself, but he can't locate his M4. The acrid scent of burning bodies was so strong, the taste of it coated his tongue.

Kage had no idea what the fuck was going on, but he knew he had to fight his way clear of it or die trying. He needed his weapon. A Marine without his weapon was almost as good as dead.

"Kage. Kage. Kage." A calm voice called to him over and over, demanding his attention. If Kage stopped to acknowledge the call, Marines could die. He battled on.

"Gunny Bennett," the voice said, with a note of command. The voice seemed familiar, but Kage continued to ignore him. "Gunnery Sergeant," he snapped, and it nearly sounded like an order.

Kage's eyes snapped open and all he saw were walls painted a dark color. He was sitting on his ass, and he had to get up, right the fuck now. He struggled against strong, unseen hands restraining him.

The screaming continued. "Marine!" the man shouted with his familiar voice, inches away from his face. "At ease, Marine. Stand the fuck down."

The direct order, given firm and loud, finally got through to Kage. He recognized the voice and knew he should respond to it. Kage stopped fighting the strong hands restraining him. His chest heaved as he breathed harshly. Christ, it sounded like he was dying.

"Kage, Kage," the voice was back, quiet and soothing now. "You gotta calm down. You were dreaming again. You're okay. You're at home, in bed, with me."

Zach.

Kage focused on the familiar sound of Zach's voice as it washed over him, calming him.

"You're fine. It was just a dream. Just relax and let me help you." Zach's voice finally dragged Kage out of the fog. He rubbed his hand up and down Kage's tense back.

Shrugging off the uncomfortable touch, Kage glanced around the room, struggling to control his breathing. The dark walls, white trim. The pale blue linens on the giant bed were bright, even in the darkness. He was in his own bed, in his own bedroom, inside the small house he shared with Zach.

"Kage?" Zach sounded concerned again. "Are you okay, now?"

"Yeah," he answered slowly, remembering the dozens of times this had happened before. "Yeah, I'm okay, now." The dreams had gotten worse, not better, the longer he was home.

"Good," Zach sighed, relief and sadness both obvious in his expression, and his voice.

"I'm good, I'm good," Kage insisted, struggling to regain his composure and slow his hammering pulse. "I'm sorry to wake you again." His throat was on fire, but now Kage realized it was because all those screams had been his own.

"Don't be stupid, Kage. It's okay to wake me if you need me," Zach replied gently.

Zach's company in his bed was comforting. As soon as that thought resolved, Kage hated himself. Zach shouldn't have his life thrown into chaos like this. He deserved to be with someone he could touch and would touch him back.

"Think you can go back to sleep now?" Zach asked.

Kage lay back down as Zach straightened the bedclothes around them. He closed his eyes and concentrated on the pleasant feel of Zach's warmth as it filled the space between them.

"Do you remember anything about your dream?" Zach asked.

"No," Kage answered in a whisper. "It's like I'm there again when I dream, but as soon as I wake up, it's blank."

"Just go back to sleep, then," Zach murmured.

Kage took a deep breath, trying to relax. The night sounds were so much louder than he remembered. The walls of their small house closed in on him. He loved this house. He loved sharing it with Zach. It had been the perfect house for the two of them, when they'd signed the lease three months ago.

They'd both been so optimistic the first six months, while Zach attended the police academy. He'd started his career on the ground floor, working a day shift in a jail. Kage had almost believed having Zach in bed beside him each night would hold back the nightmares. He'd been so fucking wrong. About so many things.

Kage didn't know how he'd managed to live this long, when so many better men had died. It was inevitable that fate would catch up with him, very soon. It was just a matter of time. Kage was suddenly overwhelmed by the knowledge that his own life was almost over. There was no way in hell he'd live to see forty.

. . .

He was so lost in his own thoughts, Kage forgot Kim was behind him. He stared at the shelf in front of him, without seeing what was on it. He wasn't even sure what-all this aisle had. Kim touched his arm as she placed something in her cart, and Kage jumped. His heart leapt out of his chest and his hand shot out to grip her wrist, hard.

"Ouch!" she gasped. After a moment's startled hesitation, she used her free hand to pat at the back of Kage's wrist. "I didn't mean to startle you. Could you please let go of me, now? Kage, you're hurting me."

Zach appeared from around the corner. Quickly but carefully, he approached Kage and Kim. "Breathe slowly," Zach encouraged. "In through your nose, out through your mouth. You're okay, Kage."

Suddenly aware of just how tightly he gripped his own sister's delicate wrist, Kage released her. His palm felt as though he'd been scalded. The skin of Kim's wrist was white. It flushed red as the blood flow returned. She'd have bruises tomorrow.

Fuck, Kage wanted to curl his hand into a fist and slam it into the shelf in front of him. Jesus Christ, what was wrong with him? He watched Kim rub at her injured wrist, her motions screamed at him like an accusation. He was such a fucking asshole. Kage had to get a hold of himself. He had to keep things like this from happening.

"I'm sorry Kim," he said, sounding stiff and insincere to his own ears. "I should know better. We're in the middle of a fucking supermarket."

"It was my fault," Kim said hastily. "I moved too fast, snuck up behind you. I didn't mean to startle you."

"Hey, you didn't mean to hurt her," Zach said, his tone placating. "She understands. We all understand." He did an awful lot of that, lately; struggle to keep Kage calm, at the same time trying to smooth things over for everyone.

Zach didn't need this shit in his life. The nightmares and hypervigilance were bad enough, now Kage was having trouble even getting into, let alone riding in, a motor vehicle. Just yesterday, getting home from a doctor's appointment had been a major ordeal.

Kage was fine, at first. He climbed into the passenger seat of Zach's small SUV, just like he always did, waiting for Zach to come around and climb in the driver's door. But once he was there, inside the car, Kage couldn't breathe. The passenger seat in the SUV suddenly looked too much like the passenger seat in a Humvee. His view out the windshield, the window to his right, they all conspired to *remind* him. Sweat broke out along his hairline.

Kage's heart was in his throat. He heard *sounds*; loud noises, screams and shouts. He could smell things. Burning bodies, blood, exploded ordinance. Kage shoved the car door back open with damp palms and trembling hands. He fucking fell out of the vehicle, wrenching his knee in the process. He braced himself against the SUV and hauled himself to his feet. He couldn't see approaching threats if he was lying crumpled on the ground.

Zach was suddenly beside him. "Kage, what's wrong? Talk to me."

"Give me the keys, Zach," he demanded. Now that he was outside of the car, his pulse was slowing, and he could catch his breath.

"What?" Zach's astonishment was glaring.

"Give me the fucking keys. I'm driving." There was no way in hell Kage was getting back into that passenger seat.

Zach's brows rose, his eyes wide with incredulity. His mouth hung open slightly, in disbelief. "You're in the middle of a panic attack, Kage. You're a danger to the other drivers on the road in this condition."

"I'm not getting back into that fucking seat." Kage's hands shook when he ran them over his face.

"Okay, that's fine," Zach easily agreed. "We'll figure something out, but you can't drive, Kage."

He obviously couldn't sit in the passenger seat of a fucking car without losing his shit, either. Kage knew he was in no shape to drive. He wanted to admit this to Zach, but he couldn't form the words. He saw no way out of this fucked up mess he'd created. Kage's unaccustomed helplessness made him want to put his fist through a window. Safety glass or no, he might be able to shred his knuckles enough to take his mind off how fucked up his life had become.

"It might work if you stretched across the backseat," Zach suggested hesitantly. It was obvious he was afraid his words would incite Kage, even though he knew he *had* to do something.

Kage peered through the window at the SUV's interior. Sitting in the backseat, however cramped, might make things look different from the way they did inside the Humvee.

Zach opened the rear passenger door. Kage carefully eased himself onto the backseat. His knees met the back of the front seat, but there was still enough room for him to sit comfortably. Kage took a deep breath, waiting for his heart to try to leap out of his chest again. Nothing happened. Kage was still in California, no images from Iraq assaulted him, dragging him back into hell.

Zach closed the car door, and Kage flinched, but panic didn't overwhelm him. The unwanted memories stayed away. Zach slowly, carefully opened the driver's door and slid into the seat. He gently pulled the door closed. Settling himself back, Kage enjoyed being able to breathe normally. Things weren't as bad back here. He could do this.

"Ready?" Zach asked, watching Kage closely over his shoulder. His smile was forced, the corners of his eyes tight with tension.

Kage hated that look on Zach; especially because he was usually the cause. He used to like it when Zach looked at him, eyes sparkling with humor. He used to kiss Zach, just to see him smile afterward.

Kage nodded his readiness. Why did Zach even put up with all of this? He deserved to be with a man who could still make him smile.

. . .

Kage was stretched out on the sofa. He knew it was early Sunday morning, but he wasn't sure exactly what time it was. Zach would be home from work, soon. Kage had polished off a six-pack, hoping it would allow him a dreamless sleep. He didn't sleep much anymore, since Zach had rotated onto the night shift at the jail.

When Kage did manage to slip under, he always woke up grasping for his weapon. On Zach's most recent night off, Kage had thrashed so much, his elbow connected solidly with Zach's cheekbone.

Voices. There were voices in the distance, but they were coming closer. Kage snapped out of his stupor, sitting straight up. He grabbed his Berretta off the coffee table, racking a round. He moved quickly, silently, through the house. He checked the locks on all the doors and windows, again. He'd already done this several times through the night, but Kage was compelled to check them all again.

The voices were coming from in front of the house. Kage pressed his back to the wall beside the front window, gun muzzle pointed at the ceiling. The blinds were closed. They were always closed. He wouldn't let Zach open them. That much unprotected glass wasn't secure.

Kage parted two slats of the blinds with his free hand. There were kids on the sidewalk in front of the house. Kage tightened his grip on his sidearm, quickly scanning the group for weapons, or any other threat. The kids were all different ages but shared the same coloring. Kage absorbed the fact they were all dressed in nice clothing, their hair neatly brushed. He checked his watch. It was just shy of 0800 on Sunday morning. A teenage girl appeared, also neatly dressed, to corral the younger kids and get them loaded up into a car.

The family next door was heading to church, just like they did every Sunday morning.

He tried to relax his white-knuckled grip on his sidearm. Kage's fingers were stiff from holding the weapon so tightly, for so long. He rested his head against the wall behind him, willing his breathing back to normal. He ran the back of one shaky hand across his forehead, wiping away the collected sweat.

Kage crossed the room and sat back down on the sofa. He slid the magazine from the Berretta, pulling back the slide to clear the round from the chamber. He pushed the cartridge back into the magazine, then reloaded the weapon. Setting it on the coffee table again, Kage sat back, hoping his beer-buzz hadn't faded.

He heard scratching sounds at the front door. Kage sat up instantly. He grabbed the Berretta and pulled back the slide. His heart was trying to pound its way through his ribcage, he couldn't catch his breath. He aimed at the still-closed door and waited to identify his threat.

The hostiles didn't immediately come through the front door. In fact, it sounded like they were fumbling with a key. The key to the front door of Kage's house.

Fuck. Zach. Zach was home from work. Who else would dick around with a key?

Kage lowered the hammer on the Berretta and slid it onto the table, just as Zach stepped through the doorway.

"Hey," Zach greeted with a cautious half-smile. His shoulders drooped, his eyes were bloodshot, with dark circles beneath them.

"Hey," Kage replied automatically, hoping Zach couldn't hear the rapid beat of his heart from across the room. "Easy shift?" He was always so glad when Zach came home. He wanted to go to him, greet him like he used to, in the very beginning. Kage wished he could endure being touched, again.

Zach snorted derisively. "A warm Saturday night at the booking facility for the entire northern half of San Diego County. You're kidding, right?"

Kage sat back on the sofa, struggling to look calm and relaxed. Zach was feeling him out, testing his mood, gauging his reactions. It had become part of their routine, after every one of Zach's twelve-hour shifts, replacing the warm greetings they used to exchange. It pissed Kage off that Zach had to tip-toe around him, constantly testing the quicksand that had become their life together.

He watched Zach set down his rucksack and hang his keys on the hook by the door.

"How was your night?" Zach asked, the neutrality of his tone long practiced.

"Same old shit," Kage growled. He was happy to have Zach home, why the fuck couldn't he make him feel welcome?

Zach crossed to the coffee table and picked up the Berretta. With quick and confident hands, he withdrew the magazine, slowly pulling back the slide. He ejected the cartridge.

"Why was there a round in the chamber?" he asked quietly.

"Because that's how the gun works," Kage snapped. "Forgetting to chamber a round can get me killed."

"I wouldn't think there's much need for a loaded nine-millimeter, in the middle of suburban San Diego." Zach disappeared into the bedroom, taking the unloaded Berretta with him.

Kage's palms itched without his sidearm. He got twitchy if he didn't have the ready protection of his weapon. "What the fuck are you saying, Zach?" Kage yelled, surging to his feet and stalking into the kitchen.

When Zach reappeared, he still wore a skivvy shirt with his olive-green uniform pants. "I'm not *implying* anything, Kage, if that's what you mean. I'm providing an opening for you to tell me if there's something wrong."

Kage pulled another beer from the fridge. He leaned heavily against the countertop as he took several long draughts from the chilled bottle. "There's nothing wrong. It's not like I don't know how to use the fucking gun. I'm a Marine, for chrissake." Kage swallowed hard against the lump in his throat. He hated fighting with Zach, but he hated thinking even more.

Zach collected empty beer bottles from all over the house, placing them into the recycling bin. The tension was palpable, but Kage couldn't say the words that would dissipate it.

He was about to step past Kage, when Zach stopped in his tracks. He reached for Kage's arm, where he pressed it to the counter, supporting his own weight. Kage tensed, knowing Zach was going to touch him. He was scared shitless, his heart crashing against his ribs. Kage held his breath.

Just as Zach touched Kage, he said, "You're bleeding. How did you hurt yourself?" Zach's expression was concerned. His voice was soothing but hinted at curiosity.

The grip of Zach's fingers around Kage's wrist was gentle, his hand pleasantly warm. Kage recoiled, trying to pull his arm free. "It's nothing," he snapped. "I'm fine." He detested touch, Kage couldn't endure it. He curled his hand into a fist, pulling steadily against Zach's grasp.

"Blood's running down your arm. Just let me have a look at it." Zach's voice was calm. His hold on Kage was gentle, but strong. It was obvious he was determined to check Kage's wound.

"It's just a scratch. I'll take care of it myself," Kage said angrily. He took a step, needing to get space between the two of them. He yanked his arm upward to break Zach's grasp. Kage needed to get Zach's hand off of his wrist. He should have changed his shirt, so his arms were covered. Zach wouldn't understand all the fresh scabs and new scars.

"Kage, relax," Zach said sharply. His expression showed his annoyance as he held fast to Kage's wrist. "I'm not going to hurt you. If it's just a scratch, then let me look at it. You'll put my mind at ease, if you just humor me."

That last part was a plea. It managed to steal its way into Kage's heart and touch the feelings he had for Zach. The strength of those feelings was as powerful as they ever had been. They were just out of his reach, these days. Reluctantly, Kage relaxed into Zach's grip.

"The bleeding already stopped," Kage said stiffly, bracing for Zach's uncomfortable questions.

Zach lovingly cradled Kage's forearm against his side, examining the darkened blood of the fresh wound. Kate gave himself a mental kick in the ass for not bandaging his arm when he'd finished this morning. He'd meant to change into a shirt with long sleeves, too.

"I'll clean it up, and throw a Band-Aid on it," Zach said quietly. He tenderly traced the scabs that lingered on Kage's forearm and wrist. "How did you do this?" he asked quietly, his touch still loving. "How come this keeps happening?"

Kage swallowed convulsively, several times. He hated Zach's hands on him. "I dunno. Working on my bike? One of our cars? Could be from work." His voice was low and strained, his words clipped. It took all his self-control not to rip his arm out of Zach's hands.

"They're too regular; too precise, to just be random and accidental." Zach danced the tips of his fingers over both the fresh, and the fading scars running from elbow to wrist. He looked up and met Kage's eyes. There was genuine confusion there, as well as worry. "There's so many of them. They look like you could have made them all with your Ka-Bar."

Kage tugged his arm backward, but Zach resisted. "It's not a big deal," he muttered. He struggled to hold Zach's gaze.

"Well, no, each cut by itself is no big deal," Zach replied softly. He covered Kage's inner arm with his palm. "But it *is* a huge deal if you keep doing this to yourself, over and over."

"I never said I did it to myself." Kage tried to get his arm back from Zach.

"Don't do that," Zach pleaded. He held fast to Kage's arm. "Please don't pretend that everything is okay." He gently caressed Kage's arm, tracing the uniform scars, and wounds in various stages of healing. "There's a reason you need to keep doing this. I'm worried about when small cuts won't be enough, anymore."

Kage started to protest. He knew what he was doing, he wasn't going to let it go any further. Zach's expression stopped him. He looked at the marks on Kage's arm with concern, not revulsion. When he looked up, Zach held Kage's gaze steadily. His eyes were warm and filled with affection.

"Sometimes, it's the only way I can get things out. It's the only way I can relax." Talking to Zach was safe and comfortable. Kage just couldn't form the words to speak them.

"I'm sad knowing something keeps you from being happy, and at peace." Zach spoke softly, as he soothed Kage's arm with his gentle touch. "But you're not defective, weak, pathetic, or whatever it is you're afraid I might think."

"I know that," Kage snapped, scowling.

"Good," Zach said quickly, his expression fierce enough to silence Kage's next protest. "And whenever there's something inside you that you need to get out, you *can* talk to me." Kage shook his head in denial, but Zach pushed right through. "Nothing you tell me will change how I see you, or what I think of you."

The room tilted. Kage breathed rapidly but couldn't get enough air. "You don't know that for sure." Some of his memories left a dark taint that Kage didn't want anywhere near Zach.

Undaunted, Zach lovingly caressed Kage's arm. His expression was open and honest; he looked at Kage as if he genuinely *saw* him. "I know what you're trained to do, and where you've been sent. But I also know why you're a Marine, and that's what matters more."

There'd been a time when Kage had loved seeing Zach with the same expression he wore now. He could remember how that expression had made him feel special. That look had the power to make Kage feel worthy and cherished. Now, he was numb. He knew those emotions were there, but they weren't his to feel. "I guarantee you, when I kick down a door and take out everyone inside who's shooting at me, I'm not thinking about *why* I'm a Marine."

"No, but you *are* thinking about the men who are going through the door with you, and after you," Zach replied solemnly. Lifting Kage's arm, Zach kissed his palm, then pressed it to his cheek. "If it was just violence and killing you lived for, you would have become a thug, and I'd be locking you into your jail cell every night."

He watched Zach nuzzle his palm, but Kage couldn't feel it. It was like seeing it happening to someone else. He yearned to cup Zach's cheek, caress his cheekbone with his thumb. Instead, Kage stood frozen. "You shouldn't have to know about the ugliness. Some of the shit people do to each other...it's dark." He swallowed hard, struggling to slow his breathing.

"I'm a cop, for chrissake," Zach said with annoyance, "I work in a jail. I've seen one man beat another man to death, just as an example to other inmates. I've seen men shanked in the shower, just because of their race. The things these guys do to end up in jail, in the first place, are pretty fucked up."

"It never seems to touch you," Kage murmured. He admired Zach's clear green eyes, open and honest as he held Kage's gaze. "You have a good heart. You're strong and pure. You shouldn't have to see all the ugliness." Mortified, Kage pressed his lips into a thin line. He had no idea why he'd blurted his thoughts like that.

Zach gave Kage a small smile. His skin was smooth, and his face seemed to have a glow. The flush on Zach's cheeks deepened, slightly. A lump formed in Kage's throat so he could hardly breathe, let alone speak. He managed to curl the fingers of one hand around Zach's. He couldn't bring himself to do what he really wanted to, though; place a kiss on Zach's full lips.

"Those things surround me, but they're not a part of me." Zach lifted their joined hands, pressing his lips to the backs of Kage's fingers. "I can listen to the things that are haunting you, without getting caught up in them." He placed kisses on each of Kage's fingers, his free hand still caressing the scars.

Kage believed Zach. He felt Zach's unconditional acceptance, and his desire to help Kage in any way he needed. Zach was a guiding star in a clear sky; bright and uncorrupted. Kage needed him to stay that same way. Confessing his acts, disclosing things he'd witnessed, would pollute their home. If Kage burdened him with any of this, it would leave Zach stained. As Zach placed kisses to his palm, Kage knew he needed sanctuary, more than he needed solace.

He couldn't help the quiet sound of discomfort that escaped him, as Kage tried to free is hand from Zach's grasp. He didn't want to give Zach the wrong idea, but he knew he failed. Kage saw the pained look of rejection, before Zach managed to mask it. Pain twisted Kage's gut.

They moved around each other in awkward silence, desperately avoiding even the smallest touch. Kage should tell him how much he needed Zach, and how much he wanted Zach's touch. Zach just made him so fucking vulnerable, just his touch threatened to break Kage.

Zach finally broke the silence. "My parents invited us over to their house, on my next Saturday off." Kage grunted a response. If he ignored the invitation, he couldn't be blamed for refusing to go.

Despite his exhaustion, Zach was going to be persistent. "My mom said she'll make that ambrosia salad you like."

There'd been a time when Kage's mouth had watered at just the thought. "Tell her not to go to any trouble."

"She doesn't consider you to be any trouble, Kage," Zach scolded gently.

"I'm not going." Kage finished off his beer. Why the fuck did Zach always force him into having to refuse? It was his fault Kage had to be an asshole.

"You can't stay locked up inside the house when you're not at work." Zach's sigh was the only sign of his frustration. "My family misses you. They'd really like to see you."

"I'm not a fucking child, Zach," Kage shouted, because he needed to. "You can't guilt me into doing something I don't want to do."

"That's not what I'm doing—"

Kage didn't let him finish. "I'm immune to your shit now, so just get the fuck off my back."

"I'm not making another excuse for you." Zach's voice was tight, his expression pinched. "*You* can call my mom and tell her why you're blowing her off. Again."

Kage slammed his empty beer bottle into the kitchen sink. Shattered glass rained down everywhere. He didn't stay to witness the fall-out.

"Fuck you, Zach!" Kage yelled. He slammed out the door leading to the garage.

He wanted to ride. The knot of fear that had taken up permanent residence in Kage's gut, always punched its way out into the world wearing a mask of anger. His motorcycle always helped. Speed, along with the isolation inside his helmet, loosened all the things that were twisted up inside of him.

Kage had stormed out without his jacket or his keys. Fuck. He sure as hell wasn't going back inside for them. Heaving a deep sigh, Kage fisted his hands on his hips, glancing around the garage. He could clean out his Jeep while he waited for Zach to fall asleep.

Hitting the button to raise the garage door, Kage headed for the small fridge in the corner. He pulled open the door with more than a little worry. He'd been sucking down a lot of beer lately, and he was lazy about keeping this fridge stocked. He blew out a relieved breath when he saw the single, lonely bottle on the top rack.

Kage pounded down the beer in a single go. He threw the empty into the trash with too much force, wincing at the sound of breaking glass. Kage needed to chill the fuck out. He had better control of himself than this.

He got the trash cleared out of the inside of his Jeep before Kage started to nod off, sitting up. He jolted himself awake, just as a strand of his own drool landed on his thigh. He wiped his mouth with the back of his hand, silently chiding himself for being a sloppy drunk. Kage had been awake all night, waiting for Zach to come home so he could sleep. It was time he got his shit together, went inside, and got some sleep.

He was probably even drunk enough that he wouldn't dream.

Kage closed the garage door, and quietly slipped into the house. He paused to listen. No music. No television. Zach had probably collapsed into bed as soon as Kage had tucked his tail and run.

The house was dim, with all the blinds closed. Inside the bedroom, Kage found Zach, just as he'd expected. The ceiling fan turned slowly, gently moving the cool air. Zach lay on his stomach, covered by a single sheet. He was curled around the pillow, as much as he was asleep on top of it. He looked at peace, despite the dark circles that were still beneath his eyes.

Kage's heart ached. He hated the distance, and the tension that was between them, these days. He hated himself for being the cause of it. Zach deserved none of this.

Slowly stripping off his clothes, Kage left them where they fell. So many bad habits had crept into his routines since he'd returned from Iraq. Kage knew he'd become an asshole, and a slob. He managed to keep things together at work, because everything was routine for him. He was on autopilot, sleepwalking through his days, and it was reflected in his latest fit-rep.

Lifting the sheet, Kage slid into bed beside Zach. He pressed himself against Zach, so clumsy, Kage was surprised he didn't wake Zach. He tucked a pillow beneath his own head, curled around Zach's body, draping an arm over his waist. Zach stirred slightly, murmuring as he pushed back against Kage's chest.

"I don't have anywhere to be until tonight," Zach whispered, surprising the hell out of Kage, "so I didn't set an alarm."

"Good. You need your sleep," Kage whispered on a sigh, his face buried in Zach's hair.

Finally catching a break, Kage didn't dream.

Their fragile truce was good. While it lasted, anyway. Kage managed to stay mostly sober, and not pick any fights with Zach, at least for a couple of weeks. Somehow, he even got a hard-on, a couple of times. Zach hid his disappointment when Kage couldn't stay hard, but Kage still knew how he felt.

He struggled to come in his own hand, these days. The bitch of it was, that was one of the only times he felt anything, anymore. Kage wasn't even sure he really felt anything, even then, or if it was just the memory of how he was *supposed* to feel. Now, as he stood in the middle of the kitchen, Kage was staggered by the realization that he'd already lived the better part of his life. He was on borrowed time now, so why the hell had he even made it back from Iraq?

The walls closed in on Kage. He was sure Death had reached up through the ground to claw at his legs and would drag him down any moment now. Zach was talking. Kage heard his voice, but he couldn't make out the words. He couldn't breathe.

Kage grabbed his keys from their hook, yanking his leather jacket from the closet. He stormed through the house toward the garage. He should tell Zach what he was doing.

"You've been drinking, Kage," Zach shouted, starting to follow. "Do *not* get on that fucking motorcycle."

Kage wasn't a little kid who needed a scolding. He answered Zach with a middle fingered salute, as he slammed out the door. Kage needed speed. He needed the sound of wind rushing over his helmet. Maybe it would drown out the thoughts racing around inside his brain.

Afternoon traffic was a motherfucker. He wove through the cars, stopped bumper-to-bumper on nearly every street. Kage drove like they weren't even there. He zigzagged between them when he could. When he couldn't, he raced along the left shoulder. He didn't hesitate to take the right shoulder when he had to. When there was no other choice, Kage drove on the sidewalk.

Anything to keep from slowing down. Anything to not have to stop.

Finally, outside of town and free of traffic, he shifted through the gears and opened up the bike's powerful engine. Everything was a blur around him. His heart pounded. Adrenaline prickled beneath Kage's skin. He reached the bike's top speed and it still wasn't enough.

Pain was the only fuckin' thing Kage was able to feel anymore. It wasn't like he was going to live much longer anyway. He'd lived the best part of his life, already. Might as well go out on his own fucking terms.

It was full dark when Kage finally pulled off the road. The rest stop was deserted, but he still parked in a dark, secluded corner. Let someone try to fuck with him. He was ready.

Kage draped his jacket over the bike's seat. He settled down on the curb, drawing his legs up toward his body to rest his arms on top of his knees. Lifting a cuff of his jeans, Kage wrapped his fingers around the familiar hilt of his Ka-Bar, pulling it free of its sheath.

He closed his eyes against the sight of headlights moving in the distance. Kage gripped his knife in his right hand, making a fist with his left. His left arm had healed enough, since the last time he'd had to do this, so Kage rested that forearm against his thigh, wrist up. He opened his eyes and contemplated the pale, tender skin.

Kage laid the blade of the Ka-Bar against the flesh of his arm, near the bend of his elbow, and drew it across. The cut was shallow, but the sting of it was satisfying. The tightness in his chest loosened. The blade was sharp and his skin parted easily. Kage was so familiar with his knife that, even in the dark, he made several cuts. Each slice cleared the gathering fog from his head. He made a neat row of them, down the underside of his arm. Blood welled up slowly, the darkness making it appear black instead of deep red. He could breathe more easily now.

His arm burned with the cuts and he *felt* it. The tension in his shoulders eased, leaving his body, along with his blood.

Re-sheathing his Ka-Bar, Kage took a deep breath. The muscles in his back and shoulders released the last of his tension. He needed to go home. He knew Zach was there, pissed off, and worried. Mostly worried.

Kage kept fucking things up, but he didn't know what he could do any different. He wanted to do what made Zach happy, he just didn't know anymore, what that was. Any choice he made, these days, was the wrong one. He wanted to feel about Zach like he used to. A part of him still knew what that felt like. Kage just couldn't find that part of himself, most days.

CHAPTER TEN

Zach was doing laundry.

Kage sat on the sofa; drinking his fifth beer, channel surfing, and ignoring Zach.

He'd told Zach not to bother with Kage's clothes. He had a large pile of uniforms he needed to drop off at the dry-cleaner, the next time he was on base. He hated the thought of Zach handling his filthy skivvies and socks, with the way Kage had treated him lately. Zach crossed the room and through Kage's eye-line. He wore a faded pair of jeans and one of Kage's old, coyote brown skivvy shirts. Zach was so handsome. He was tall and broad shouldered. Some part of Kage still found him stunningly attractive. He still admired Zach's smooth skin, and his pretty eyes. Zach's muscles were never obvious until Kage got him out of his clothes. He used to really like to do that, too. Deep down in Kage's brain, something still wanted to shove Zach down onto the floor, strip him naked, pin him down, and fuck into him.

Those old feelings were still there. Kage knew they were. It was just, whenever he reached for him – like now – they danced backward out of his reach. It wasn't fair to Zach. Kage's gut turned, knowing he was the one putting Zach through this. Kage wished fate would get its shit together and come claim him, so Zach would be free. Kage wasn't going to get the life with Zach he'd thought they would have, that first magical night on the beach in Puerto Vallarta. His borrowed time was almost up. They'd missed their one chance, but that didn't mean Zach couldn't move on, find someone worthy of him.

"Are you sure you don't want me to do your laundry, along with my own?" Zach asked quietly, yanking Kage from his thoughts. "Honestly, I don't mind."

"I feel like an asshole when you do things for me, I'm capable of doing for myself." Kage was surprised by his own honesty. He'd even managed not to sound hostile, or defensive. "I don't want you to feel like I think you're my maid, or something."

"I appreciate that," Zach replied, smiling. "But in this case, I'm doing laundry anyway, and adding yours to mine doesn't create more work for me." He shrugged.

"Okay, I guess," Kage said reluctantly. "If you're sure. I appreciate it, thank you." He meant that, sincerely. It was good that he remembered to say so. Maybe he wasn't as fucked up as he thought he was.

"Do you want to go out to dinner tonight?" Zach's voice startled him. Kage had been lost in his own thoughts, he hadn't noticed Zach come back into the room.

Kage shook his head in the negative. Fear grabbed him in its icy grip at the thought of spending even a few minutes inside a loud, crowded restaurant. All the strange people making sudden movements, all of the noise, was too much to handle.

"Someplace small and quiet." Zach was persistent. "We can get a table in a corner, you can face the room."

Kage's answer was to finish his beer.

Zach approached Kage slowly. He sat gently on the coffee table, facing Kage. He leaned his elbows on his knees and sighed heavily. Kage's heart hurt, remembering that day in Puerto Vallarta, when Zach had sat before him in an almost identical way. He'd been so hopeful, back then.

"You don't want to go anywhere. Besides work, you don't do anything except sit around here, and drink beer. You avoid people, including your own family." Zach's voice was soft, but Kage could hear his pent up pain and frustration. "You don't touch me anymore, and I don't dare touch you. Please do something about it. Please."

Kage was fine. He didn't need Zach pushing him to get to some arbitrary level of 'healed' before he was ready. He glanced in Zach's direction, at the same moment Zach looked up. It was on the tip of his tongue to tell Zach to stop being such a drama queen, but the look in Zach's eyes stopped Kage cold. The pain he saw there, the pleading, left him feeling gut-punched.

He'd never been any good at expressing his feelings with words. With Zach, Kage always used touch to show what he felt, and even to smooth over his own fuck ups. That way was closed to him, now. He still wanted Zach's touch, he just couldn't stand to feel it anymore. Kage couldn't stand for anyone to touch him. He ached to reach out to Zach and tell him all of this, using only his hands. Instead, he curled them into fists at his sides.

"That place on the corner, with the burgers you like," Kage stopped at the rough sound of his own voice. He cleared his throat and started again. "If we go early, before it's crowded, while it's still light, we can get a table outside."

Zach's expression morphed to hopeful but guarded. "Good. That's great. It's perfect." It seemed he wanted to say more but thought better of it.

Kage wondered when, exactly, Zach had learned to quit while he was ahead?

. . .

An explosive sound woke Kage from his troubled sleep. He threw himself from the sofa, onto the floor, grabbing the Berretta from its place on the table. He racked a round before his shoulder hit the floor. Pain exploded in Kage's shoulder, rocketing up through his neck, and down the length of his arm.

He was under attack. Kage gripped his weapon with both hands, trying to identify the threat. Loud noises were coming from behind the house. He combat-crawled along the floor, ignoring the stabbing pain in his shoulder. Kage knew he'd been hit, but he'd deal with it later. Now, he needed to neutralize the threat.

Diesel engines roared. Sounds of thunderous percussion carried across the small backyard. Kage's head filled with the sounds. They echoed and reverberated through him. He had to make it all stop.

Kage pressed himself against the wall next to a window. The sounds carried in through that window. He parted the blinds briefly, spotting a large vehicle on the other side of the short fence. There were men out there, he saw them moving around. They were the source of the loud, crashing noises.

He didn't think he could take them out from here, with just his side arm. He had to get closer. Kage needed to sneak across the small yard, but he was alone, wounded, and there was no one to lay down cover fire.

Pressing his back tight to the wall, he considered his options. Zach would be here soon. Kage had to take out the threat before Zach got here. He had to protect Zach, keep him safe.

Kage snorted a laugh at the absurdity of that thought. Zach was a cop; he could fucking handle himself. Maybe if Zach got here soon, he could provide cover. Kage could really use Zach's help, right now.

Like a beautiful avenging angel, Zach suddenly appeared in front of him.

"Kage, Kage," he said quietly, firmly, "Kage, it's okay. You're safe. Give me the gun, Kage." Zach knelt before him, careful.

"I'm hit," Kage bit out, through clenched teeth.

"Okay, okay," Zach soothed, "But it looks good, though. You look fine now. Give me the gun, Kage."

"We're under attack," Kage's chest heaved with every breath, and it was hard to speak. "It's an ambush."

"It's garbage collection, Kage," Zach said, palms out in supplication. "You're at home and we're both safe. No one's coming for you. You're safe, Kage. I'm here with you, and I'm safe. We're both okay. Now, give me the gun."

It was hard to hear Zach's voice, over the sound of his own thundering heart. Kage thought about it. He was in his own home. He glanced at his shoulder and didn't see a wound. He listened closely to the sounds from outside. The diesel engine wasn't a Humvee. The crashing sounds weren't of combat. *Fuck.*

Kage let Zach take the Berretta from his numb fingers. He tried to swallow, but his mouth was dry and his throat was tight. He began to struggle to his feet. Zach reached out to help.

"Don't touch me," Kage yelled, shoving Zach's hands away. He levered himself up against the wall.

Kage was losing his fucking mind.

Zach set the Berretta on a nearby table and turned back to Kage. "Come on, let's go sit down. I'll get you some water."

"Fuck the water, I need a beer," Kage barked.

"You don't need beer," Zach argued, his expression darkening. "I suspect beer might have been a factor in your overreaction."

Kage couldn't believe he'd mistaken fucking trash collectors for armed hostiles. He was better than that. "You don't know a fuckin' thing about it," he snapped at Zach.

"I know more than you think, Kage," Zach said sharply. "You thought you were under attack from the trash men. You had a loaded gun in your hand, trying to figure out how to kill a couple of innocent civilians."

"I was in a defensive position," Kage argued lamely, running trembling hands through his hair. "I wasn't on the offensive."

"I'm afraid of what would have happened if you'd had a clear shot," Zach reached toward Kage. "Now come on, let's go sit down."

"Fuck off, Zach."

Zach's hand wrapped lightly around Kage's bicep. Kage curled his other hand into a fist. "Get the fuck off me!" he roared, as he aimed his blow. Kage's fist landed squarely against Zach's jaw. Zach stumbled backward, releasing Kage, but he didn't go down.

Of course he didn't. It would take more than a blow to his chin to bring Zach to his knees.

Kage stood frozen, unable to say the words he knew he should. He watched, detached, as Zach dabbed at his lower lip and checked for blood. There was none, and Kage felt a modicum of relief. It wasn't going to stop a bruise from blossoming on Zach's jaw. Remorse settled over Kage like a heavy blanket, his shoulders sagging from the weight. Things had gone too far, finally. No way should he have ever considered Zach a threat. Kage was out of control.

When he spoke, Zach's voice was low and dangerous. The tremor it held was the only indication of his barely contained rage. "I've tried to be patient and understanding, Kage. But you've gone too far, this time."

Kage pushed away from the wall. Zach backed up several steps. Kage flinched. His legs were like rubber. He wasn't sure his knees would hold him much longer.

"I'm gonna go lie down." Kage indicated the bedroom door.

"Yeah, I think you should," Zach agreed.

Kage stumbled into the bedroom and collapsed onto the bed. He lay back, throwing an arm over his eyes.

He had no idea how much time passed before Zach came into the room. Kage lowered his arm. He knew Zach wasn't going to let him hide behind anything while they had this talk.

Zach sat on the edge of the bed. He held a bag of frozen peas to his jaw, where Kage had hit him.

"You need to get help, Kage," he said simply, and quietly. "You've developed a short temper. You're jumpy, and you startle easily. You've lost all interest in everything we used to do, and everything you've told me you enjoyed. You can't sleep, you have nightmares. You drink way too much, and you're a nasty drunk. You're hyper-vigilant now, and you just experienced a flashback."

Kage could only nod at the truth of Zach's words.

"You just hit me," Zach continued, ominously. "We're in a romantic relationship, and we live together, Kage. You realize what it means, that you hit me?"

"Yeah, I do," he said morosely, his voice rough. Kage should probably apologize, but he had a feeling it wouldn't make any difference at this point. He'd be lucky to stay out of jail, and he was already on thin ice with his command.

"You carry a loaded handgun around the house, and you just hit me. I can't live like this, Kage. I *won't* live like this."

Kage's stomach turned sour. He knew what came next. He wished he had his Ka-Bar right now, the comfort of the familiar grip in his hand. He needed to get the tension out with a few long slices to his arm, just so he could make it through hearing Zach's next words. Kage remembered just how much Zach meant to him, now that he'd gone too far.

"I've asked you to get help, before. Now I'm telling you." Zach leaned over Kage, forcing Kage to look him straight in the eye. "Get help, or I'll have you arrested, and I'll move out. It's not an ultimatum. It's a promise."

Kage could only blink. Zach had given him a choice.

"If you can't get into the VA soon enough, we can find a private therapist. I can get the name of one who works with our department, since there's a lot of a similarity, between law enforcement and the military."

"Yeah, okay," Kage agreed readily, reaching desperately for the olive branch Zach extended. "That's a good idea."

Zach nodded, his expression losing some of its tension. "If we have too much trouble with the VA, I'll register you as my domestic partner and get you onto my health plan."

Kage started to protest, then realized nothing was more important than Zach. There was nothing to argue about.

"If neither of us can get our benefits to cover it, I'll start working overtime to pay for it," Zach declared plaintively. "Whatever it takes, Kage. You get the help, you do the work, and I'll take care of everything else."

Kage wasn't worth all of this heartache, he was putting Zach through. Zach seemed to think he was, though. Zach was pretty fucking smart, so Kage thought it might be time to listen to his advice.

"I'm afraid it will take time for it to get better." Kage wasn't quite sure what he was trying to say.

"Yeah, I'm sure it will," Zach replied quickly. "I expect it to. All I ask is that you do the work, get the help. Progress, not perfection."

"Think you can stick it out long enough?" Kage managed to ask through clenched teeth.

Kage saw a flash of pain in Zach's eyes just before he squeezed them shut. His shoulders sagged. "I miss you, Kage. I'll stick it out if there's any chance I can have you back."

Kage nodded his understanding. Speaking was impossible past the lump in his throat.

"Can I touch you?" Zach's question surprised Kage.

He realized how much he missed Zach's touch. Kage was suddenly very sad that he was so fucked up that Zach had to ask permission to touch him, or risk injury.

Kage opened his arms. Zach rested his head against Kage's chest, gripping his shirt tightly. At Zach's first touch, Kage remembered how much he enjoyed this, and just how long it had been since he'd had it. Kage wrapped his arms around Zach's shoulders, breathing deeply. He caught the scent of Zach's hair and recognized yet another thing he missed.

This was the closest thing to peace Kage had felt, in months and months. Zach's warmth was comforting, his weight was reassuring. Zach clung to Kage, almost desperately. He wondered, suddenly, how much pain he'd caused Zach, without ever laying a hand on him.

CHAPTER ELEVEN

Zach's parents walked them to the front door. Kage suspected it was more than just a case of good manners; they had missed these visits and wanted to make it last. Guilt made Kage's throat tight, which happened a lot lately. Now that he didn't have to fight so hard, just to make it through each day, Kage clearly saw how much he'd retreated from his own life. All the people in their lives that he'd desperately avoided for so long, didn't hide just how damn happy they were that Kage was a little better, these days. Zach's parents had felt especially rejected, and Kage regretted that.

"Mom, don't crowd him," Zach said gently. With a hand on her arm, he encouraged her to put a little space between herself and Kage.

The front door was at his back, so Kage opened it. Immediately, his tension receded, and Kage's need to escape eased. "It's okay now," he said, gesturing toward the open door. He even managed a small smile.

"I don't mean to be pushy," said Zach's mom. She managed to look both chastised, and eager. "It's just I've always liked to show my love with hugs."

Kage breathed. His therapist had taught him some exercises to help control his anxiety, and they enabled him to get through times like these, without losing his shit. "A hug is okay," he said, opening his arms. "Just give me a heads up, so it's not a surprise." The therapist said this would eventually fade, too. Like with everything else, he had to keep working on it, and give himself time.

Zach's mom stepped into his embrace, squeezing him tight around the waist. Kage smiled at her enthusiasm, feeling slightly goofy at how giddy he was from just a hug.

"That means you can't just launch yourself at him, whenever you feel like it," Zach's father said dryly, frowning slightly at his wife's back. "Remember, he's not Zach."

"I know, I know," she replied, waving an impatient hand at her husband, as she pulled out of Kage's arms.

"Yeah, well, she doesn't even launch herself at me, anymore," Zach said with feigned resentment. "My mom loves Kage more than me, now."

Zach accepted his mother's effusive hug. They all laughed, which felt strange to Kage, at the same time it felt pretty fucking great. He held out his hand for Zach's father to shake, bidding them both goodnight. He stepped out onto the front step, as Zach finished saying goodbye to his family.

The neighborhood was quiet, as they walked to their car. Kage took a deep breath, enjoying the chill of the air in his lungs, and let it out slowly.

"Are you okay?" Zach asked. He couldn't quite hide the concern and tension in his voice. Things were a hell of a lot better between them than they had been, but they still had a long way to go. Kage knew it would be a while before Zach stopped waiting for the other shoe to drop, always sure he was just a moment away from losing his shit again.

"I'm good," he replied reassuringly. Tentatively, Kage gave Zach's shoulder a squeeze. "Just working through some shit. I'm a little tired."

"I'm not surprised," said Zach. "You lasted several hours, which is amazing. My parents are probably celebrating, right now." He chuckled quietly. "They missed you."

Kage suspected it was Zach's smile his parents had missed, but he kept that thought to himself. He disarmed the car alarm, and they both climbed into their seats. Kage should probably say something to Zach, to let him know he was aware of how hard he made things between them. He didn't mean to, but his therapist said it might help them both, if Kage acknowledged it.

They were silent on the drive to the freeway. Once he was up to speed, Kage cleared his throat nervously. "Your parents know I couldn't help how I felt, right?" he asked carefully. "They don't think I was just a dick, and refused to visit them, do they?"

"No, no one thinks you were just being a dick," Zach reassured him quickly. "We all knew you were struggling—that you're still struggling—with issues. Nobody was pissed off at you, we were all just worried."

Kage snorted in disbelief. "There were times I *know* I pissed *you* off, no matter how hard you tried to hide it."

"I was never pissed at you," Zach denied vehemently. He looked over at Kage, expression aghast. "I understand what's going on, and why. I know you weren't always in control of it. But you're working on getting better."

Kage shook his head. He resisted the urge to accept Zach's denial and move on, cause then he'd be a chicken shit. "You understand, but it used to piss you off just the same, when I couldn't go out into a crowd." He tried to wet his lips, but his entire mouth had gone dry. "It still makes you mad when I can't talk about the fucked up shit in my head." He was sure Zach seethed silently when Kage's dick failed to work—*again*—but he still couldn't even talk to his therapist about that.

"Yeah, I'm angry at the situation." Zach shrugged, looking out the passenger window. "But I don't get angry at you. I hate that your own brain and body hijack your life, and there's not a fucking thing I can do."

Kage thought back over all the times Zach had reached out to him, sometimes begging him to talk about the things that tied him up in knots. For the longest time, his own emotions had evaded him. He sensed them, sometimes Kage thought he could touch them, if he reached out. But he didn't really *feel* anything, right up until he felt everything all at once, and it only released its hold on him when he cut himself open.

"You help," Kage said, barely loud enough to be heard over the hum of the car engine. He took a deep breath to gather his strength, but he exhaled shakily. He sensed his control slipping again, his shoulders lifting, and his back tightening with rising tension. Christ, he was never going to get his shit together, was he? He was on borrowed time already, why the fuck didn't his life just end, so Zach wouldn't have to suffer through this misery anymore?

"Hey. Where'd you go?" Zach's calm voice cut through Kage's thoughts, jerking him back into the present. "We were talking, and you just faded out. Everything's okay. Nothing pressing in on you." Kage nodded stiffly, starting his breathing exercises in earnest. He backslid so fucking quick, still. He should probably be grateful he could drag himself back out now, almost as quickly.

"Can I touch you?" Zach's tone was deceptively casual. Touching was still like a walk through a minefield, for them. "Just your hand, or your leg. For comfort."

Kage tried to answer, but his voice wasn't working. He cleared his throat. "Yeah. Yes. That's a good idea." He rested his arm on the center console.

Zach was paying close attention, like he always did. Kage exhaled with relief when Zach's hand settled on top of his, gripping gently. Kage squeezed in return, not caring if it seemed like he was clinging. They'd lost this, for a while, and he'd missed it. He should tell Zach how much he'd missed it, and how glad he was they could touch each other again.

"You do help," Kage managed to say, his voice rough. "It doesn't seem like it, I know. But you do."

Zach gave Kage's hand another squeeze. "Good. I'm really glad to hear that."

"There've been times when I woke up in the middle of the night, in a panic." Kage swallowed hard, his throat suddenly tight and painful. "And then I felt you in bed next to me, and sometimes I could even smell your scent on the sheets, and the panic went away."

"It makes me happy to know that." Zach's voice was low, but he sounded sincere.

"I know I'm not easy to be around, most of the time." Kage took a couple of deep breaths, struggling to stay calm long enough to say what he needed to. "I know I put you through hell. You should have dumped my sorry ass a long time ago. But I'm glad you didn't. So, I'm trying." He'd managed to say what he wanted to say. Whatever else happened, he'd accomplished that.

"You're doing more than trying," Zach surprised Kage by saying. "You're succeeding. Every day, I see you conquer something else. Lately, it's been like having the real Kage back, and I'm glad I stuck around for that."

Kage was glad, too. Except he was painfully aware that he wasn't all the way back to his old self. "Not exactly how you pictured things would be, when we left Mexico," he said darkly.

"And you had all this planned out?" Zach chuckled, and Kage smiled at the sound. He'd missed Zach's smiles, and his laughter.

"You know..." Kage paused, searching desperately for the right words. "You know...nothing...none of this had anything to do with you. It was all me. It *is*...all me."

Zach was silent for a long while, staring out the passenger window. Kage tried not to read into the silence, like his therapist advised him.

"My head knows that," Zach finally said. "But my heart doesn't have the same firm resolve."

"Yeah, I get that," Kage said on a heavy sigh. "My body is still being hijacked. I'll get back in line with my head...and my heart." He took another steadying breath. He'd reached his limit for the night, Kage just hoped to hell he'd said everything he should say to Zach. He wondered if it was too much to hope that he'd said everything Zach needed to hear.

"Well then," Zach said slowly, as if choosing his words carefully, "all the more reason to stick around, I guess, to see how this all turns out."

Kage gave Zach's hand a squeeze, to let him know he'd heard. He couldn't trust himself to say anything else. It didn't matter, though; Zach kept his hand on top of Kage's. They made the rest of the drive home in a comfortable silence.

CHAPTER TWELVE

Kage held a set of briefs and sleep pants in his hand, ready to put them on and slide into bed. He caught sight of one of his scars. He had a lot of them now, from all the cutting he'd done. Some of them were pretty ugly, but they weren't hideous to look at. Some of them were still an angry red, but like all the others, they would fade until they were smooth and pale.

Fuck it. If Zach wasn't bothered by the sight, Kage was done worrying about them. Zach looked at Kage's scars with concern, but never with revulsion. On the rare occasions, these days, they were naked around each other, Zach didn't focus on the scars. Kage always felt Zach saw him completely, admiring him with appreciation – and no small amount of desire.

He tossed his clothes back into their drawers, sliding between the sheets naked. It felt good. Kage hadn't slept like this since ... well, in a very long time. He was about to shut off the bedside light, when Zach padded quietly into the room. He gave Kage a significant look, one side of his mouth lifting in a hesitant smile, before slipping into the bathroom.

Kage couldn't remember that last time he and Zach had gone to bed at the same time. He left the light on so Zach could easily find his way across the room when he was ready.

Zach emerged from the bathroom, completely naked and semi-hard. Kage was surprised. It had been a long time since Zach had been that blatant in his nudity. Kage's pulse kicked upward slightly.

His cock stirred between his legs, in a way it hadn't in a long while. He watched Zach slide into bed beside him. Kage reached for the lamp switch, but Zach stopped him.

Swiveling his head on the stack of pillows, he watched as Zach settled on his side, facing Kage. He propped several pillows beneath his head, and searched Kage's face closely, that half smile lifting one side of his generous mouth.

"You going to bed early, tonight?" Kage asked the obvious.

"I thought I'd try," Zach replied. "That all right with you?"

Kage felt the warmth of Zach's body seeping into the sheets. "Yeah, that's fine."

"The doctor took you off the anti-depressant a month ago, didn't he?"

"About that, yeah." Kage wondered about Zach's query. He knew better than Kage, what medications he'd been weaned off of.

"How are you feeling without them?"

"As good as I did with them," Kage answered truthfully, thinking of all the things that held his interest these days; all the activities he and Zach participated in, again. They'd been jet skiing, recently. They'd started going to restaurants and bars together, again, enjoying each other's company, like they used to. They'd even visited Kage's family for an afternoon.

"Without the frustrating side effects, maybe?" Zach asked, shifting slightly closer to Kage.

"Are you thinking of one side effect in particular?" Kage couldn't help his smile. He felt himself stir with interest, remembering how good it used to feel to press himself against Zach's body.

"Absolutely," Zach replied as his expression fell into serious lines. "Unless it's not the side effects that's been the problem."

How in the hell could he be asking that? Especially when he justifiably could have turned his back on Kage, long ago. He skimmed the backs of his fingers along Zach's cheek, pleased when his eyes widened in surprise. "None of what has been wrong with me, ever had anything to do with you."

Zach looked hesitant, like he was unsure he could believe Kage. "We had problems long before you started taking anti-depressants. I know it's a common symptom of PTSD, but..." He gave a negligent shrug with one shoulder.

It had been so damn hard for Kage to talk about this with his therapist. Zach deserved the truth, but it didn't make it easier to say the words. "I have always wanted you, just as much as I did the first moment I saw you. I just ... lost touch with myself, for a while." Holding Zach's gaze for several long moments, Kage hoped he'd see the truth.

"It's been lonely here without you," Zach said softly. He gave Kage a tremulous smile. Exhaling a shaky breath, Zach looked away, blinking rapidly. Kage lay with his arm on the bed between them, Zach tracing his fingertips over the linear scars that ran from wrist to elbow.

"You could have left," Kage whispered. "You *should* have left. I'm just grateful you didn't."

"I knew the Kage I met in Mexico was in there somewhere. I had to be here when we finally found a way to let you out." Zach had barely finished speaking when Kage crossed the space that separated them. He clutched at Zach, bringing their mouths together hard.

Zach's answering kiss tasted of desperation. He cradled Kage's face and licked into his mouth. Zach tasted good. Kage spanned Zach's ribs with one hand, kissing him back, hard. This felt right. It felt like it used to, not like the awkward false starts they'd given up on in the recent past.

Kage pressed himself flush to Zach's heated body. He ground their cocks together when Zach pushed back. Zach was hard against Kage's hip. He breathed against Zach's open mouth, wanting more. Kage wanted more than he'd wanted in a long time.

Zach slid a hand down between their bodies, wrapping his fingers around Kage's slowly-hardening cock. It was a welcome sensation, and Kage fucked himself into Zach's fist. It had been a very long time since Kage had been able to feel something close to arousal. His own hand on his dick might coax a partial hard-on but coming had become a struggle. He'd just quit touching himself all together, while he'd been on the medication.

Tonight though, Zach had his full attention. If Kage could get all the way hard this time, he wasn't going to last long.

"I've fucking missed you," Zach whispered against Kage lips, so quiet, he almost didn't hear it.

Kage silently agreed, with his whole heart. He hoped his sluggish physical reaction didn't give Zach the wrong idea.

"How 'bout I provide a little added encouragement?" Zach asked, already pushing back the bedclothes and sliding his body down the length of Kage's.

Zach slipped between Kage's legs and sucked his dick with enthusiasm. The wet heat was just as good as Kage remembered. The pounding pulse of blood rushed into his cock with each glide of Zach's mouth. He kept growing, longer and thicker, after he thought Zach had encouraged everything from him. Kage felt Zach's lips on him, really felt it. He'd been numb for so long. Moving restlessly, Kage silently asked Zach for more.

He got his wish when Zach released his nearly-hard cock with a lewd, wet pop, and shifted to take one of Kage's balls into his mouth. Kage moaned encouragement, loving Zach's lips on his sac, his tongue lapping at each of Kage's balls in turn. Zach pressed Kage's legs upward, lowering himself to tongue Kage's hole.

Kage chuckled breathlessly. "I fucking love your tongue."

Zach's answer was to lick into him, lap at him, run his thumbs over Kage's opening. "Do you want to come like this? With my mouth?"

"I want to be inside of you," Kage blurted.

Zach surged upward, pressing his chest to Kage's. They kissed, wet and messy, while Zach jacked him, with firm, slow strokes.

"How should we do this?" Zach husked, pressing his forehead to Kage's, chest heaving with each breath. "What would be easiest for you?"

Fuck. Would Kage's problems always cast a shadow over their every contact? "This seems good." He indicated their current positions. "Or on our sides?"

"Yeah," Zach said, sitting up suddenly. "We can try it this way. You're relaxed, right? It's better when you're relaxed."

Zach didn't wait for Kage to answer. He leaned to the side and pulled out the drawer of his bedside table. He withdrew a fresh bottle of lubricant and a condom, setting them on the bed. Zach moved sensuously against him, until he straddled Kage's chest.

Kage's eyes locked on the foil-wrapped condom, and his entire body tensed. He picked up the offending object, running his thumb over its smooth surface thoughtfully. He and Zach had visited a clinic, when they'd gotten back from Mexico, and hadn't used condoms since. They both knew Kage had been too screwed-up in the head lately, to fuck around.

It had to be Zach, who'd found someone else. As sick as it made him to think about it, Kage couldn't blame him, and he shouldn't be surprised.

"Hey," Zach said sharply, snatching the condom from Kage's fingers, and with it, his attention. "It's been a while, for both of us. This is just to help it last long enough for us to really enjoy it." He smiled, and it lit his entire face. "I'll take all the help we can get."

The painful tightness in Kage's chest eased. He smiled his appreciation up at Zach as relief washed through him, and all the tension fled Kage's body. He wasn't going to have to spend the entire time worrying he would come too fast and leave Zach unsatisfied. Because Zach was still his; he'd waited for Kage, despite the many months of bullshit.

Kage reached for the lube bottle and tore away the plastic wrapping. "Can I do this?" he asked breathlessly, "Or do you need to?"

"You give it a try," Zach replied, steadying himself with a hand on the headboard, "and we'll see how it goes."

Kage coated two fingers, then slid his hand between Zach's thighs where they straddled his chest. He watched Zach's face closely, as he slid one finger into this body. Zach's eyes fell shut, his expression smoothing out, then suffusing with pleasure. His cheeks flushed, his brows knit in a frown, and his mouth fell slightly open. That was the look Kage remembered, the one he'd hoped to earn again.

Zach moaned softly, low in his throat. He pushed against Kage's hand slightly, and clenched tight around his finger. Kage stroked his finger in and out, pushing it to the last knuckle. He twisted slightly, spreading the lube carefully.

Gently, he added his second finger. He watched the corner of Zach's mouth lift in smile. He stared down at Kage with heavy lidded eyes.

"Fuck, that's good," Zach sighed.

Kage slid three fingers into Zach's clenching hole. He crooked one of them, pressing easily into the gland he found unerringly. The result was immediate and gratifying.

Zach slapped another hand onto the headboard in reaction. "Don't fuck around like that," he said on a mirthless laugh. "It's a struggle to hang on, as it is."

Kage chuckled in answer and pressed his fingers deep. Zach gasped when he drew them out to add more lube. His body opened right up, this time.

"Are you ready?" Kage asked, tongue thick in his mouth. "It's been a while, so I don't want to rush you."

Grinning suggestively, Zach eased himself carefully down Kage's body. His movements were slow and deliberate. It hurt like hell to see Zach's lingering hesitance, each time he wanted to caress Kage. He'd fucked everything up between them, by losing track of his feelings for Zach, his need for Zach's touch. It hovered between them, like a specter, and probably always would.

"I'm ready for you," Zach said with a growl. "I've been ready for you for a long fucking time." He tore open the condom packet, reaching for Kage's cock.

Pushing away his dark thoughts about the future, Kage focused on Zach, anchoring himself to the present moment, like he should have been doing all along. He covered Zach's hands with his own, stilling his movements. "I'd better do that. If I let you, this might be over before it gets started."

Handing over the condom eagerly, Zach watched in avid fascination as Kage rolled it onto himself. Kage added more lube to his sheathed cock. It had been so long for both of them, he wasn't going to take a chance on hurting Zach with too much friction and drag.

Zach sank down onto his erection and Kage forgot how to breathe. He watched Zach's face closely, memorizing each expression, and knowing what he did that caused it. Kage would never know how Zach could look ethereal and debauched, at the same time.

They moved against each other slowly. Zach fucked himself on Kage's cock, his motions steady and measured. Kage was eager and tactile, running his palms up Zach's thighs, then skimming over his ribs. Zach sank down, taking all of Kage deep inside his body. Kage wrapped his hands around Zach's ribcage, feeling like he'd found a lifeline.

He remembered the early days; the first few crazy weeks when they'd fucked like their lives had been on the line. Zach used to abandon all control to him, and Kage pushed them both to their limits. He wished to fucking Christ they could both just let go, and fuck like they used to.

Kage drew his knees up, pressing his feet flat into the mattress, and they found a rhythm. Zach rode Kage's cock at a furious pace, Kage pushing up into him, getting as deep as he could.

He watched Zach watching him, as they moved together. Kage gripped Zach's ribs, knowing he would leave bruises. Zach wrapped his hands around Kage's biceps with an equally tight grasp. Fuck, Kage had missed this. He'd missed Zach's heat enveloping him. He'd missed the loud, sweaty meeting of their bodies. He'd missed the sights and sounds of Zach coming.

Kage silently thanked Zach for thinking of the condom. He was on the razor's edge of coming. If not for Zach's strategic planning, he probably would have shot his load already. He wanted to last longer, he *needed* to last longer, so that Zach would be sated and happy.

"You okay?" Zach grunted between hard thrusts. His rhythm faltered slightly as his expression grew pensive.

"Fuck yeah," Kage breathed. "You feel so fucking good."

"So do you. Christ, I love your cock." Zach emphasized his words by tightening his body around

Kage, deep inside of him. Expression softening, Zach lightly caressed a hand down Kage's chest

"I wanna make you come," Kage said as he wrapped a hand around Zach's straining erection.

Zach twined his fingers with Kage's. Together, they stroked Zach's cock. He watched Zach finally let go and give in to the pleasure. He kept his own expression honest and open, leaving himself vulnerable and at Zach's mercy.

"Fuck, I'm close," Zach groaned, never looking away from Kage's face. He always did that before; let Kage see everything. He knew Kage wanted to see everything.

Zach's entire body tensed. All motion stopped. Kage held his breath as he watched and waited. Zach's mouth fell open in a silent cry of pleasure. Kage didn't dare blink. Zach tightened his fingers in Kage's grip, still wrapped around his cock. Kage's erection was gripped in the tight heat of Zach's body as he came. Hot splashes of thick come landed on Kage's belly and chest. He felt each rolling wave of Zach's climax in his dick, as Zach's body clenched all around him.

Kage braced his hands on Zach's chest when he toppled forward, finally released from the grip of his orgasm. He laughed self-consciously, and Kage knew he was giddy with pleasure. Zach braced himself with a hand on either side of Kage.

"I haven't come like that in ... a long fucking time." Zach's chest heaved with each breath.

Suddenly, he sat up, rising off of Kage's cock with a hiss. "Fuck! Easy, easy, easy ... oh fuck," Kage protested.

Zach shushed him as he rolled the condom off of Kage's sensitized dick. Tossing it aside, Zach sank down, taking Kage back into his body.

The heat that enveloped Kage was scalding. He couldn't help pushing himself upward, hard and fast. It didn't take any more than three or four thrusts, and he was coming inside of Zach.

It slammed over him, fast and hard. His fingers clenched tight at Zach's hips. Kage's eyes slammed shut on their own, and he saw lights dancing across the backs of his lids. His orgasm rolled through his hips and settled, almost painfully, low in his gut. For several long moments, Kage's body didn't feel like his own.

When Kage could move again, Zach eased off of him. Kage struggled to catch his breath. For the first time in longer than he could remember, Kage felt at home in his own skin.

When Zach disappeared into the bathroom for a warm, wet cloth, Kage got up and retrieved two bottles of water from the kitchen. He was able to take care of Zach again, to look after his needs. Kage accepted that it would take some time before Zach would feel secure enough to submit to him again. He'd show Zach he was ready, though, while he waited.

Kage stood passively, drinking his water, as Zach cleaned him of their combined sweat and come. When he was done, Kage pulled him in for a kiss. They reassembled the bed and climbed back in together. Kage shut out the light. He lay in the dark, listening to Zach breathe, feeling the heat of his body permeate the sheets.

"Can I touch you?" Zach whispered into the dark.

"You don't have to ask that anymore, Zach," Kage answered gently. "We're past that, now."

Slowly, cautiously, Zach snaked an arm around Kage's waist. Kage opened his arms and drew Zach closer to him. Zach rested his head on Kage's chest. He caught the scent of Zach's hair; a little like his shampoo, a little like his sweat, but mostly Zach. Kage inhaled deeply, shutting his eyes and just savoring.

In Kage's arms, Zach relaxed against him completely. He collapsed, boneless, into the bed. It was a complete release of tension, and something Kage hadn't felt Zach do since ... well ... it felt like since forever.

Kage sighed, letting himself relax along with Zach. He smiled into the darkness when Zach's breathing evened out, and he began to snore lightly. He pulled Zach closer, finally relaxing enough, he knew he could sleep. Kage would escape insomnia tonight. With Zach wrapped around him, he might even get away without a nightmare. Best of all, he and Zach could touch each other again. He might have been *wounded* for a time, but Kage had not *broken*.

TRADEMARKS ACKNOWLEDGMENT

The author acknowledges the trademarked status and trademark owners of the following wordmarks mentioned in this work of fiction:

Pacifico: Cervecería del Pacifico, SA de CV

Corona: Cervecería Modelo, SA de CV

San Diego State: The Trustees of the California State University

Humvee: AM General LLC

M16: Colt Defense LLC

Jeep: Daimler Chrysler

Band-Aid: Johnson & Johnson

Ka-Bar: KA-BAR Knives, Inc., subsidiary of Cutco Corporation

ABOUT THE AUTHOR

Kendall McKenna was the **MLR Press Author of the Year for both 2013 and 2014.** Her second novel, **<u>Strength of the Pack,</u>** was nominated for a **2013 Bookie Award, by Author's After Dark.**

Her first work of fiction was written at the worldly age of nine and was a transformative work that expanded on the story told in a popular song of the time.

She tried her hand at vampire and cowboy fiction, winning high school poetry and short story contests along the way. It wasn't until she discovered the world of m/m erotic fiction and found her stride with cops, Marines and muscle cars, that she felt inspired to share her stories with readers who enjoy the same things.

Putting herself through college by working in a newly created HIV testing clinic in her local Department of Health, introduced Kendall to the gay and lesbian community. Understanding and empathy has made her a lifetime advocate of GLBT issues.

A brief bout of unemployment gave Kendall the time and focus she needed to finally produce a novel worth submitting for publication. Her first novel, **<u>Brothers In Arms</u>**, introduced the world to her authentic military stories and characters.

After breaking an ankle in a freak incident, Kendall battled an extended case of writer's block. She also blames her character "Terrell", and his reluctance to be the center of attention.

Kendall was born and raised in Southern California. COVID caused some upheaval that resulted in a necessary move to Louisiana. Her small dog enjoys it when she writes, as she sits still long enough for her to curl up beside her.

You can find Kendall on the internet at:
Facebook: www.facebook.com/kendallmckenna
Instagram: AuthorKendallMcKenna

KENDALL MCKENNA

Email: kendall.mckenna3@gmail.com